O

MW00761959

Dust
Aftermath
Sidecar
Bottle Rocket
A Christmas Tree Grows in Baltimore
Hoosier Daddy
Three

by Salem West

Hoosier Daddy

by Barrett

Balefire
Flights of Fancy
Windy City Mistletoe

June Magee, R.N.

FESTIVAL NURSE

Ann McMan

With Salem West and Barrett
Original Illustrations By Biz

BInk

Bink Books
Bedazzled Ink Publishing Company • Fairfield, California

978-1-939562-80-7 - paperback
978-1-939562-81-4 - ebook

Cover Illustration by
Biz

Cover Design by
TreeHouse Studio

Excerpts from *Hallowed Murder* by Ellen Hart. Seattle, WA :
Seal Press, 1989. Reprinted by permission of the author.

Bink Books
a division of
Bedazzled Ink Publishing Company
Fairfield, California
http://nuancebooks.bedazzledink.com

This book is lovingly dedicated to Tereska Torres,
Vin Packer, Ann Bannon, March Hastings, Joan Ellis,
Claire Stanley, Valerie Taylor, Della Martin, Paula Christian,
Monica Nolan, Mabel Maney, Kay Johnson, Brigid Brophy,
Sloane Britain, Sheldon Lord, Nan Keene, Marjorie Lee,
Kay Addams, Carol Clanton, Vicki Evans,
Ann Summerhill, Wilene Shaw, Tony Trelos,
and all of the other pulp fiction writers who paved
the way for the stories we now are able to tell.

We thank you for your expressions of humor,
vision, determination, and courage
at a time when our world was not as
warm and welcoming a place.

ACKNOWLEDGMENTS

From Ann McMan

One of my favorite pastimes is to troll the aisles of our local *Lost In Time Antique Mall*. Over the years, I've discovered countless treasures. Authentic Pennsylvania oilcans, a vintage Steel Pen display case, old mark Jugtown pottery, odalisque-shaped boot jacks (it's a long story), rustic pieces of furniture, tin cooking utensils, and, of course, the books. Those wonderful old, illustrated books that brought back vivid memories of all the happy childhood hours I spent living out wondrous and epic adventures with the likes of Nancy Drew, Trixie Belden, and, of course, Cherry Ames, R.N. Those sweet, fantastic tales added a depth and richness to my life that I have never forgotten. As a way to say thank you, I thought it would be great fun to revisit the art form and give it a contemporary twist. Enter June Magee, R.N.

I owe a huge debt of gratitude to my beloved Lodge Sister, Jeanne Barrett Magill, for keeping me on the straight-and-narrow as I hammered out a modern-day incarnation of an age-old classic. Her experience and expertise in the profession, as well as her good-natured indulgence of my many narrative excesses, proved invaluable. Nurse? I owe you.

I'd be remiss, too, if I didn't mention the valuable editorial role undertaken by my wife, the august Salem West. Together, we crafted every detail of the story. Each step of the way, she corrected, questioned, encouraged, nudged, and improved the writing of this book. It is by no means an overstatement to say that her fingerprints are all over June—in a spousally approved way.

What can I say about Fay Jacobs? She is a great friend, a good sport, and a legendary talent. Without her help and oversight, this book would not have been possible—at least, not without endless litigation and a plethora of restraining orders. If angels walk the earth, they surely love martinis, Miniature Schnauzers, and a place called Rehoboth Beach.

Thanks, too, to the great Ellen Hart for allowing me shamelessly to quote from her first Jane Lawless classic, *Hallowed Ground*. In time, biographers may view this concession as her greatest lapse of judgment.

Lynn Ames, Jessie Chandler, and Michelle Brooks? Your royalty checks are in the mail….

Sincere thanks, as always, go to Casey and Claudia at BInk. You continue to be our steady hands and guiding lights. Thank god you never get tired of our "great" ideas.

Last but not least, the fantastically talented Hayden "Biz" Sharpe brought June and her cohorts to life through her lively and spot-on illustrations. Thank you, Biz, for your talent, your professionalism, and for being this writer's "Boz." The world is just opening up for you. Be sure to pack plenty of pen nibs and clean underwear for the journey.

From Salem West

The *Rule of Three* is a writing principle that suggests that things that come in threes are inherently funnier, more satisfying, and more effective than other numbers of things. After working on this project with Ann McMan and Jeanne Barrett Magill for lo these many months, I can unequivocally say that I concur.

Ann's writing, even in the festive cloak of pulp fiction, wields a metaphorical church key that opens up a wonderful world that is broader than two women falling in love, richer than a small cadre of supporting characters, and more colorful than witty dialogue. And, Barrett's patience and sage advice on the outer limits of the nursing profession added not just legitimacy to this endeavor, but also a strong fashion sense.

A special thanks also goes out to Biz Sharpe, who made this

book all the more special with her steady hand, keen eye, and amazing talent.

And, I would be remiss if I didn't say thank you to Jennifer Shylanski and Rebecca Brenowitz for letting me read all of their books, even if I got the bedroom with no heat.

I love you all.

From Jeanne Barrett Magill

It was with much joy and gratitude that I had the opportunity to brainstorm with the amazing Ann McMan and Salem West at an IHOP over some breathtaking blueberry pancakes, crispy bacon, and a large pot of coffee. The result was our shared dream to craft this pulp fiction homage to that most perfect icon of nursing: June Magee, R.N.

Pages of notes, tears of laughter, a modicum of superb wine, and a compendium of hideous diseases bore fruit. My humble responsibility was to act as technical director and medical vestments advisor.

I want to thank Ann and Salem for their humor and brilliance. I'd also like to thank Jean Balke, Admissions Director at Augustana Hospital School of Nursing for taking a chance on an older student who burned with fire in her belly to become a nurse. Over the past thirty-five years, I have cared for thousands of our "broken and bleeding," and it is my fervent hope that my excellent training benefitted some of them. I offer a heartfelt salute to all of my sisters and brothers in white.

Suffer little children to come unto me, and forbid them not: for of such is the kingdom of God.

—Luke 18:16

CHAPTER ONE
Under the Boardwalk

"DORRIE! GET YOUR ass in here."

Cold coffee.

He hated cold coffee. He hated a lot of other things, too.

He hated summer. He hated this damn heat. He hated the fact that the air conditioning on the top floor of this damn building only blew lukewarm air. He especially hated the asshole who labeled the elevator button for his floor "13." It was no accident that this happened on the day *she* first walked in.

That nurse. That effing, goody-two-shoes in white stockings.

Max hated her most of all.

And he had good reason.

Max Markham was editor-in-chief of the *Windy City Mercury*—one of the oldest and best independent newspapers in the country. He'd been sitting in this chair for nine years now. And during that time, the paper had won three Pulitzers and had been instrumental in toppling an organized crime syndicate that made IBM look like a corner car wash.

But it wasn't enough. Every day, his subscription numbers dropped faster than the temperature of Lake Michigan in February. It was clear that if something drastic didn't intervene, the *Mercury* would soon be on the auction block.

But not anymore. Not since that day two years ago when some fat asshole choked on a piece of gristle during the lunch rush at Ralph Lauren's frigging steak house on Chicago Avenue. And did the jerk have the decency to die? No. He was "saved" by the ministrations of Max's nemesis, June Magee.

Correction. *June Magee, R.N.*

And, of course, Oprah was off her diet that day, so she

witnessed the whole damn thing. And could she just give her a goddamn Pontiac and send her on her way?

No. She put her on her show and offered her a fat book contract. Then the wife of his publisher got the great idea that Crack Nurse should write a regular column for the paper. *His* paper.

Next thing he knew, Nurse Ratched was an overnight sensation.

Now he was stuck with her . . . probably for life. And those flagging subscriptions? He looked down at the daily tracking report. They now were through the goddamned roof.

Yeah he hated her. She was a celebrity now. A superstar. A goddamn cultural icon. And as a result, he'd had to add an entire staff of people just to manage her effing PR tours. Her breakout self-help book, *What Would June Do?* was still topping all the best-seller charts. And her weekly column by the same name had single-handedly pulled this newspaper from the brink of bankruptcy.

She was one royal pain in his ass. And it didn't help his plight when Oprah's magazine makeover whackos got their mitts on her and turned her into goddamn Rita Hayworth.

That was the final insult. Florence Nightingale was built like a brick shithouse—and was just as unobtainable.

He scowled and sniffed at his cold coffee.

"Dorrie!"

Where the hell was that lame-ass admin of his?

"I'm on the phone, asshole!" his assistant, Dorcas "Dorrie" Douglas yelled from her adjacent office. "Get it yourself."

Max glared at his open doorway.

Why didn't I become an orthodontist like my cousin?

He deliberated about just flinging the cup of coffee across the room, but that never worked out for him. The last time he tried it, most of the liquid landed on his desktop computer and fried the motherboard.

"You wanted to see me, Max?"

Rodgers. *Great.* At least he could get that taken care of.

Max Markham

"Yeah." He waved a hand toward the only chair in his office that wasn't covered with stacks of paper. "Siddown. We've got a new assignment for you."

"Sweet." Rodgers entered the room and plopped down into the chair. "I was about ready to chew off a leg to get out of following those damn aldermen around. Whattaya got in mind?"

Max stared at his best news photographer. Too bad the kid drew the short straw. But bad news was best when delivered like ripping off a Band-Aid.

"How do you feel about trains?"

"Trains?" Rodgers looked confused.

"Yeah. Something wrong with your hearing? *Trains.* As in, travelling by train to reach an end point."

"We're doing a story about trains?"

"No. Why the fuck would we do a story about trains?" This was getting nowhere. "I need to you travel by goddamn train to cover a story that waits at the end of the line." Max chuckled. That actually had a kind of film noir ring to it. Maybe they could use that in the coverage? Smokin' Hot Ice Nurse and Androgynous "Boi" Photographer strike out. People loved all that smoldering, sexual ambiguity. Hell. If they leveraged it right, these two could be the new *Rizzoli & Isles.*

Christ. He was starting to think like the goddamn publicist.

Clearly he needed more meat in his diet.

Roi Rodgers was staring at him with suspicion.

"What?" Max barked.

"Just what kind of story are we discussing, here?"

"For starters. We aren't discussing anything. I'm telling you what your next assignment is. You can either take it, or spend the next month covering the Windy City Wedding Show at McCormick Place. Your choice."

"Wedding show?"

"Yeah. Word on the street is that the new fabrics this year are a stunning departure from the norm." He gave Roi a minute to absorb that detail. "Kinda makes you throw up in your mouth a little bit, doesn't it?"

Roi blinked. "So what's at the end of this train ride?"

"Magee is here!" Dorrie bellowed from the outer office.

Roi's eyes grew wide. "You cannot *fucking* be serious?"

Max shrugged.

"I have a Pulitzer."

Max shrugged again.

"In *news* photography."

"You're breakin' my heart, Rodgers. You think I *like* having to cover the public appearances of this damn Diphtheria Dolly? As long as her column sells copy, I gotta suck it up and deal with it. So if you ever want a shot at running that international desk you're always droning on about, you'll wise up and learn how to be a team player."

Roi didn't get a chance to reply because the doorway filled up with a blinding flash of white.

June Magee, R.N. had arrived.

"You asked to see me, Chief?"

Magee had a voice like an alto sax. That part always rattled Max, who thought she should sound more like the tinny horn on that '68 Karmann Ghia she drove.

"I don't think you've met Roi Rodgers yet, have you?" Max gestured toward Roi, who was staring up at the vision in white with an open mouth.

"Why no, I haven't had that pleasure." June shifted her impressive bundle of assets to face Roi, who belatedly climbed to her feet. "I've certainly admired your work." She extended a manicured hand.

Roi took hold of her hand but still seemed unable to find her tongue. June towered over her by at least six inches. Roi's eyes were about level with June's clavicle. She was having a hard time keeping her gaze from dropping down to stare at the impressive swath of real estate that swelled out just below it. Instead, she nodded stupidly.

Max rolled his eyes. "Clean off another chair, will ya, Rodgers? I need to talk with the two of you about your next assignment."

*"Well, dust off your tongue depressors . . .
it's time to hit the bricks."*

"Oh?" June fixed Roi with a brilliant smile. Her blue eyes glowed like polished chips of lapis lazuli. "Are you going to be my new photographer?"

"Yes!" Roi and Max replied in unison.

June looked back and forth between the two of them.

Max chuckled. "Roi here has just been telling me about how all the photographers compete to see who gets to travel with you."

"Really?" June sat down and crossed her impossibly long legs. The ridiculous white hose she wore made them glow like they were internally illuminated. "How sweet. I feel very spoiled."

Roi cleared her throat.

Dorrie Douglas walked in carrying a file folder. She handed it to Max.

"Here are the available dates for the next promotional tours."

"Oh." June smiled at Dorrie. "Travel time again? I feel like I only just got back."

Max opened the folder and scanned the sheets of paper inside. "Well, dust off your tongue depressors . . . it's time to hit the bricks."

"I know." June smoothed a crease in her short, white skirt. The tight fabric clung to her upper thighs like a wonton wrapper. "But all this time away is so hard on Zinka."

"Zinka?"

June looked at Roi. "My cat. I named her after my favorite opera singer."

"Zinka Milanov?"

"You know the opera?" June asked with surprise. Her voice was half an octave higher.

Roi appeared to be even more flustered. "I go from time to time."

"How wonderful. We'll have to share stories."

"I don't really have any stories," Roi stammered. "Not about that, anyway."

Max frowned at the duo. "Do you two mind if we get back to the matter at hand?"

"Of course not, Chief." June folded her hands neatly in her lap. "I apologize. But it's so unusual to meet a young man who appreciates the opera. I let my enthusiasm carry me away."

"Boi," Roi said.

June gave her a perplexed look. "Excuse me?"

"I'm not a man. I'm a boi."

"A boy?" June patted Roi on the forearm. "No, dear. You may feel a tad inexperienced, but you're quite the dapper young man."

Roi rolled her eyes and looked at Max for help.

Max shook his head. "You're on your own, kid."

"Do you still need me?" Dorrie asked. "I'm up to my ass in alligators out there."

"Yeah." Max waved a hand at her. "Where are those fucking darts?"

June sighed and closed her eyes. Max knew she hated it when he cursed. And that just made him want to crank it up.

"What darts?" Dorrie looked around the room. "Why can't you keep up with shit?"

Max sighed. Why did he put up with this bad-tempered bitch?

Probably because she was married to his cousin—the orthodontist.

"The darts. You know . . . as in dartboard darts?"

"You mean these, Chief?" June unfolded her long frame and strode across the room to retrieve a handful of brightly colored darts that were all sticking out of a large wall poster. It depicted a kitten hanging by one paw from a tree limb. "Hang in there," it read.

June handed the darts to Max, feathers first.

"Thanks," he said gruffly.

June smiled at him and reclaimed her seat.

Max hefted one of the darts before swiveling around in his

chair and flinging it toward a giant wall map of the United States. It sunk into the wall with a sharp thwack.

"Where is it?" he barked at Dorrie.

"Where is what?" Dorrie replied.

"The goddamn dart." He jerked a thumb toward Roi and June. "Because that's where we're sending these two Einsteins for their next assignment."

Roi stared at him without saying anything.

June tsked. "Oh, Chief, really. You know that's hardly a scientific method."

His beleaguered assistant sighed and walked over to the map. She took off her glasses and squinted at the tip of the dart.

"Well?" Max demanded.

"It's in the Atlantic Ocean," she said.

"So what?"

Dorrie glared at him. "You want to send them to the Atlantic Ocean?"

"Of course not. What's the nearest goddamn town?"

Dorrie squinted at the map again. "It looks like someplace in Delaware . . . Rehoboth Beach?"

"Rehomo Beach?" Max thought about it. Then he snickered. "*Perfect.* Get Fay Jacobs on the phone."

JUNE WAS HAVING trouble concentrating. And that was unusual for her.

The train for Philadelphia didn't leave Union Station until tomorrow evening, but she was already prepared. Her uniforms were pressed and hanging in the garment bag with her navy blue cape. She'd also checked and restocked the contents of her red leather nurse's bag—a special Jimmy Choo creation made especially for her. The bag also contained her trusty Merck Manual and a fresh supply of dental dams.

She smiled. That cagey curmudgeon, Max, thought he was pulling the wool over her eyes by sending her to this location.

But she was savvy enough to always research the venues for her appearances, and her findings this time suggested that the female prophylactics might come in handy for attendees at the somewhat eclectic women's festival in Rehoboth Beach.

Her shoulder bag contained her best fountain pen, a fresh supply of nibs, and the paperback copy of a mystery novel Letty lent her. They would be welcome companions on the long train ride.

Yes, everything was ready—but, still, she felt antsy and unsettled. Why? She'd done dozens of these trips before and had her preparations down to a science. And it wasn't like a long weekend at the coast would be an unwelcome change from the hustle and bustle of her teaching job at Rush St. Luke's Hospital and her journalistic responsibilities at the *Mercury.*

Still. Something was bothering her.

She looked around her tastefully, but modestly appointed Ravenswood bungalow. Everything was in perfect order. Zinka was dozing on her favorite windowsill, catching the last warm rays of the late afternoon sun.

She tapped her fingertips against her leg in agitation.

Maybe watching some television would be a nice distraction?

She was nearly halfway through the first season of her favorite Netflix series, *Orange is the New Black,* so she decided to watch another episode. She glanced at her watch and pondered. Maybe she'd even have time for two episodes? Of course, she could always watch The Discovery Channel. Sometimes Zinka was even tempted to leave her perch beneath the window and stare at the wide screen with her—especially during Shark Week. June normally watched more esoteric programming—when she took time to watch television at all. But now that she had such a public persona, she understood the importance of remaining abreast of trends in popular culture. Besides, she found the exercise of learning about the quirky goings on inside a federal women's correctional facility to be most instructive—and oddly enjoyable.

Right now, however, even the high stakes antics of female inmates in an upstate New York prison weren't enough to wrest her from her haze of distraction. Halfway into the episode, she decided that the strawberry and kale smoothie she'd made for dinner hadn't quite taken the edge off her hunger. She stopped the television. Piper and Alex were in the shower together, and those scenes tended to last a while, so it seemed like a good place to pause so she could make a light snack.

The hot air popcorn popper was a relic that she'd had since her days in nursing school, but it still worked just fine—although the roar it made was tantamount to a freight train crashing through the center of her kitchen.

Trains.

She felt her agitation increase. *Maybe some Milk Duds would be good with the popcorn?*

June kept a special stash of the wicked indulgences in a large box on the floor of her pantry. She bought them in bulk at Costco, and only allowed herself to partake of them when she felt especially pressured. Or when she was unduly fractious and distracted, like this evening.

She was counting out a modest portion of the candies—only one serving—and dropping them onto the hot popcorn when random thoughts about tomorrow's seventeen-hour train ride with her new photographer intruded on her once again. She lost count of the hard chocolate morsels. She sighed and started counting again from scratch.

One. Two. Three . . .

Roi Rodgers was such a fine-looking young man. Perhaps it was inappropriate for Max to send him on such a long journey with her. After all, they'd be thrown much together—and June was very attentive to public perceptions of propriety. Not that she didn't trust herself . . . or Rodgers.

Four. Five. Six . . .

He was probably perfectly well behaved. But at the same time, he was such a handsome man with his wavy, dark hair and hazel eyes. And she guessed he was probably pretty popular with the ladies. More than once she caught him looking at her legs with something that seemed to go beyond casual interest. Well beyond.

Seven? Six? Eight?

Not again.

She sighed and looked down at the bowl of hot popcorn where she'd been dropping the Milk Duds. They were halfway melted now.

She gave up and dumped the rest of the box into the bowl.

She was halfway back to her chair in the living room when she heard the kitchen door open.

"Yo? Clara Barton? Where are you?"

It was Letty Lewis, her next-door neighbor and confidant. Letty also took care of Zinka whenever June had to travel.

"I'm in the living room, Letty." June set the bowl of popcorn down on a small table that sat between overstuffed chairs. "Come in and join me."

Letty sauntered into the living room and dropped down on one of the chairs. She took in the frozen image of two naked women in a shower stall that was still displayed on the TV screen.

"Oh, nice." She waved at it. "Now that's what I call performance art."

June blushed and snapped up her remote control.

"I was just doing some research for my trip." She turned off the television.

"Really?" Letty's brown eyes grew wide. "So Max is finally sending you to a women's prison? It's about time. I always knew your book would be a hot seller there." She chuckled. "Although I think *Who Would June Do?* might be a more appropriate title."

"Letty. Stop it."

"Well, well." Letty helped herself to a handful of popcorn. "I see you're mainlining the Milk Duds. Who is it this time?"

June blinked at her. "What do you mean?"

"Oh, come on." Letty batted her eyes at June. "The only

"Well, well." Letty helped herself to a handful of popcorn. "I see you're mainlining the Milk Duds. Who is it this time?"

time you break out the heavy artillery is whenever some buff bit of yard bird trips that trigger lurking downstairs in your lower forty-eight."

June sighed. "I do wish you'd speak English."

"When you get the hots for someone."

June opened her mouth, but no sound came out.

"Am I right?" Letty smiled and dropped back against her chair. "Of *course* I'm right. I'm always right when it comes to your libido. You have a tell, Clara Barton."

"I have no idea what you're even talking about."

"Riiiight."

"Letty . . ."

"Okay. Forget it. Where are you off to, this time?"

"Delaware."

"Delaware?" Letty looked confused. "What the hell is in Delaware?"

"It's a woman's festival. It's on the coast. I'll be appearing at the opening session."

"Woman's festival?" Letty considered that for a moment. Then June could see enlightenment spread across her features. "Rehomo Beach?"

June rolled her eyes. "It's *Rehoboth* Beach. And, yes, that's where the festival is being held. I gather it's an annual event?"

Letty chuckled. "Perfect."

"That's just what Max said. Why is it perfect?"

"Oh, god." Letty was still laughing. "You're so fucking clueless."

"I really wish you'd quit using so much profanity, Letty. It's not very ladylike."

"Yeah? Well, neither are shower scenes in women's prisons. So I guess we have a stalemate."

June sighed. Again. Letty could be so relentless. "Will you take care of Zinka for me?"

"Of course. How long will you be gone?"

"Just four days. Plus one day on each end for travel."

"Six days." Letty fished her iPhone out of a front pocket

and pulled up her calendar app. "Got it." She looked at June. "Who's going along with you this time?"

June did her best to sound indifferent. "It's one of the paper's best, young photographers. I'm very honored that Max is sending him along."

"Really? What's his name?"

"Roi Rodgers."

"Rodgers?" Letty choked on a piece of popcorn. "You mean Roi the Boi?"

"What?" June was genuinely confused.

"Roi the . . . oh, never mind." Letty cleared her throat. "Yeah. You should be honored, all right. Roi's pretty smokin' hot."

June colored. "That's *not* why Max is sending him along."

"No doubt."

"Letty . . ."

"Forget about it." Letty pointed at the bowl of popcorn. "Eat your Milk Duds."

June shook her head and picked up another hot, chocolate-covered cluster.

"And, Clara?"

June looked at her.

"You might want to take along a few of those extra boxes of these you have stashed in your pantry."

"What ever for?"

Letty chuckled again. "Just call it a hunch."

CHAPTER TWO
Ridin' the Rails

UNION STATION WAS a zoo.

And that was pretty incredible, considering it was Wednesday.

Wednesday. Good god. They didn't even have to be at the damn "festival" until Friday night. But Nurse Goody Proctor refused to fly, so Dorrie booked them both on this effing terror train to Philadelphia.

"Why do I have to ride with her on the train?" Roi complained to Max when she found out about the travel arrangements. "Why can't I take a plane and just meet up with her there?"

"Because I fucking say so."

"Max . . ." Roi started to argue.

"Kiss my ass, Rodgers. My paper, my rules."

Roi wasn't willing to give up so easily. "It doesn't make sense, Max. Seventeen hours on a train is ridiculous."

Max took a long drag on his cigar and blew the smoke into Roi's face.

"You know what doesn't make *sense*, Rodgers?" He didn't wait for Roi to reply. "That goddamned nurse-shaped boil on my *ass*. That's what doesn't make sense. And anything that prolongs the amount of time I don't have to deal with her is just fine with me."

"I still don't see why I have to ride along with her . . ."

Max grabbed a sheet of paper off his desk and waved it in the air. "Because train fare to Philadelphia costs two-hundred-and-seventy-six bucks—compared to five-hundred-and-thirty bucks for airfare." He crumpled the paper and tossed it back to his desk. "Why the fuck are we still *having* this conversation? Don't you have some packing to do? Get the hell out of my office."

So here she was, schlepping her suitcase, backpack, and all three of her camera bags through this vaulted maze of rude and shopworn travelers. God. She'd never seen so many screaming kids and tattoo-covered vagrants in her life. This was like being stuck inside a Hitchcock movie. She kept looking around, expecting to see Cary Grant and Eva Marie Saint.

Of course, if memory served, those two ended up having some . . . interesting . . . interactions on their long train ride.

Not that she was expecting anything even remotely like that with Nurse Goody.

God. The woman was a total freak.

She thought again about how June looked yesterday in Max's office and amended her assessment. *A drop-dead gorgeous freak . . . in white stockings.*

Roi shook her head. Why were those things such a turn-on?

She must be watching too many reruns of *Emergency!* on Netflix. Truth be told, Julie London looked pretty hot in her antiseptic duds, too.

But seventeen hours on a damn train? That had to be against the Geneva Conventions.

Dorrie said she got them roomettes. She had no idea what that was supposed to mean. But in her experience, anything with the suffix "ette" attached to it had to be bad.

Barrette. Vinaigrette. Bassinette. Even *sextet.*

All bad.

Roi thought back to some of the more eclectic celebrations she'd engaged in at the party following her Pulitzer win. Yeah. *Especially sextet.* That was some particular weirdness that she had no desire to repeat. Ever.

She saw the signs for the Metropolitan Lounge and boarding area for the Capitol Limited—the train that would carry them seven-hundred-and-fifty-eight miles past moonlit cornfields and depressed, rust belt towns to the 30th Street Station in Philadelphia. Fay Jacobs said she would have a driver waiting for them there, and they'd travel the remaining distance to Rehoboth Beach by car. She had no idea how long that leg would take.

Leg. That got her thinking about Nurse Goody again.

The entrance to the lounge was just ahead. Roi could see some kind of commotion going on inside. There was a good-sized cluster of people crowded together in one area, and it looked like they were all trying to get a look at something. They were bobbing up and down and straining their necks to see around each other. She thought she saw a few, quick flashes of bright white whenever the tangled mass of arms and legs parted enough to show whatever was the center of attention.

June Magee. It had to be. The pop culture nurse was like a media magnet. Of course, that outfit of hers was hardly discreet. Roi didn't understand why she insisted on wearing it every damn place she went. Oddly, that was the one quirk about her that didn't seem to bug Max. Roi figured that Max was enough of a businessman to know that there was a direct relationship between the size of the crowds she attracted and the number of morning editions that would fly off the shelves of the newspaper racks.

She dropped her bags and fished out a camera. This reception screamed photo op, and photo ops were exactly why she was tagging along on this outing. Why not get this party started?

A redcap approached her.

"Are you traveling on the Capitol Limited, sir?"

Roi sighed. She was used to the pronoun. It was just a lot easier to shine it on. "Yes, I am."

"Would you like to check those bags?"

"Why not?" Roi hefted one of her camera bags up onto her shoulder. "All but this one."

"Yes, sir. Just show me your ticket, and I'll take care of these for you."

Roi pulled the ticket out of her breast pocket. The redcap checked it and handed her a receipt for her bags. "You got a first-class booking here. That means you get dinner in the dining car." He punched her ticket and handed it back to her.

"These bags will all be waiting for you. You'll board right over there, through them double doors." He pointed toward the back of the lounge. "I hope you enjoy the trip."

"Thanks." Roi gestured toward the crowd. "Any idea what's going on over there?"

The redcap smiled broadly. "Yes, sir. That famous nurse is here—that one that saved Oprah's friend? And she's traveling to Philly on the Limited." He was piling up Roi's bags. "I think lots of folks is gonna sleep better in them little bunks tonight, knowing she's on board."

Oprah's friend? Roi thought about correcting him, but gave up on that idea. It was pointless. Even *Snopes.com* would find it impossible to separate truth from fiction when the subject was the iconic June Magee.

"I think I'll go get a few pictures."

"Yes, sir. I don't blame you for that, no ways. She's one fine-lookin' woman."

The redcap wandered off, still stealing glances at the vision in white.

Roi worked her away around the perimeter of the crowd and started taking photos. June was smiling and shaking hands. People were holding up their cell phones and stealing snapshots. One or two people in the crowd actually had copies of her book, *What Would June Do?* They were clamoring to get close enough to her to ask for autographs. It was incredible.

Roi kept shooting. Through the camera lens, June Magee looked . . . natural. Like she was born to do this. She seemed to exude poise and calm—as if being mobbed by a throng of admirers was just another routine part of her day.

She remembered the time she met the famous soprano Renée Fleming, after a performance of *La Traviata* in Houston. She wasn't there as a photographer, but waving her *Houston Chronicle* credentials did get her backstage when no one else was permitted past the security station at the rear of the hall. She waited for most of an hour for Fleming to emerge, and when she did, her demeanor stunned Roi. The singer had

Roi Rodgers

just finished a marathon performance—nearly three-and-a-half hours, and most of that time, she had been on stage. Afterwards, she'd had to make nice with dozens of Houston's A-list, muckety-mucks. She *had* to be exhausted. Yet when she walked into the small anteroom and saw Roi waiting there, she immediately dropped her bags and her bouquet of about nine dozen red roses onto a nearby table, and walked over to give her full attention to one more, starry-eyed fan. It was incredible. Poise like that couldn't be faked—it flowed out of Fleming like a warm stream of honey. Roi never forgot that.

And she knew she'd never forget how June Magee looked right now, either. It was the same thing—that same, super-sized amount of *genuine* that you couldn't manufacture or cough up on demand like so many red carpet celebrities.

June was kneeling now, talking with a little boy. He appeared to be five- or six-years old. He was having a hard time making eye contact with her. He spent more time staring at the tip of his strobe-lighted Spiderman shoe. His left arm was in a cast. His mother was standing beside him, holding a red Sharpie marker. June gently extended her hand and touched him beneath his chin. He raised his eyes to her face.

Snap. Roi clicked the shutter.

That was the shot. That was the one that would empty all the *Mercury* racks tomorrow morning. And that's precisely why Max had sent her along on this damn roller coaster ride.

Roi shook her head and backed off to wait for June to finish signing the boy's cast.

The P.A. system roared to life and a tired-sounding voice announced that all first-class passengers on the Capitol Limited were now invited to board. June looked up toward the sound and noticed Roi for the first time. Roi saw her expression change. Her composure seemed to vanish. She dropped the marker and fumbled for it, which caused her to bump heads with the little boy. He went down with a thunk and started to cry. June looked panic-stricken, but the boy's mother waved her off with a smile.

Roi decided it was time to step forward. She pushed her way through the crowd that was now starting to dissipate.

"I think this is our cue," she said to June, who was now on her feet. "Are you ready to rock and roll?"

June gave her a confused look.

"I mean are you ready to board?" Roi clarified.

"I didn't see you arrive."

"I know." Roi held up the camera. "I got some good shots of you making nice with your coterie of admirers."

June blushed.

"Don't be embarrassed. It's part of your job."

"My job?"

"Sure." Roi waved a hand to encompass the crowd in the lounge. "Your job as a media icon."

June smoothed the skirt of her white uniform. "I'm hardly an icon, Mr. Rodgers."

Roi sighed. "Just call me Roi. It'll be a lot simpler."

"All right. Roi."

Against her will, Roi felt a subterranean jolt of something vaguely like excitement when June repeated her name. The feeling was disturbing and thrilling all at the same time. She did her best to ignore it. She wasn't positive about many things, but she knew with absolute certainty that this particular road led to only one destination: disaster.

"So." Her voice cracked, and she paused to clear her throat. "The redcap told me that we get supper as part of our fare."

"That's true." June seemed to be regaining some of her composure. "Have you ever dined on one of these trains?"

Roi shook her head.

"Well, you're in for something special. They usually go full out. China. Crystal. Wonderful cuisine. It's the perfect prelude to a restful night's sleep."

Roi wasn't ready to share her optimism. "I think that last part remains to be seen."

The P.A. system roared to life once again—last call for first-class travelers to board.

"Oh, dear. I think that means we'd better shake a leg."

It took a Herculean effort for Roi not to drop her gaze to June's shapely gams, but somehow she managed. She hefted the camera bag up onto her shoulder and offered June her spare arm. "Shall we?"

June smiled and gingerly took hold of Roi's arm. Together they passed through the big double doors to the platform where the towering, blue-and-silver Capitol Limited hummed on the tracks. Two massive engines sat in front of a line of shiny rail cars that extended the length of a city block. Roi was unprepared for the raw power the great machine exuded at such close range. It was a monster—and it's endless queue of coupled club, sleeping, and sightseeing cars looked just like . . . *diners*—hopped-up, supercharged, silver diners. On wheels—an awe-inspiring spectacle that stopped her cold. She knew she looked ridiculous standing there slack-jawed—like some kind of backcountry hayseed, seeing a motorized car for the first time.

June gave a gentle tug on her arm. "Are you nervous?"

Roi shook her head. "No. I'm . . . stunned."

June looked perplexed. "Why?"

"I don't know." Roi shrugged. "It's just so much bigger than I expected."

June looked up at the monolithic engines. "They're smaller than most airplanes."

"True. But you don't normally see airplanes at eye level—at least, not like this."

June nodded. "To me, they're like great, serpentine chains that link us to a bygone era."

Roi looked at June, wondering if she understood the irony of her observation. The expression on her face gave nothing away.

"Do you mind if I grab a few photos?"

June released her arm. "Of course not. You should. It's a sight worth remembering."

Roi looked her up and down. She was certainly right about that. "Would you mind walking toward the train?"

"You want me in the pictures?"

"Absolutely. The two of you belong together."

June gave her a blank look.

"Just trust me," Roi explained.

"All right."

A porter leaned out the doorway of one of the cars and waved an arm at them.

"You folks wanting to board?"

June waved back. "We'll be right there." She regarded Roi. "We'll board once you get your photographs?"

Roi nodded. "I just wish I didn't feel like Anna Karenina."

June laughed. The silvery sound drifted out along the platform.

"I think we're safe to expect a happier outcome."

Roi wasn't sure she agreed, but decided it was best not to argue the point.

June walked away, and Roi framed her retreating, white form against the imposing backdrop of the leviathan train. They fit together like two missing pieces from a Victorian puzzle. A nurse iconoclast and the penultimate symbol of industrialization: two misfits managing to find connection and relevance in a world that no longer cared.

ONCE ABOARD, JUNE and Roi were ushered directly to their table in the Limited's posh dining car. Several other travelers were already seated and enjoying their first round of cocktails. At least, Roi assumed they were their first rounds, because she certainly intended to have more than one. And that was especially true if anyone expected her to try and sleep on this moving metal convoy.

She was worried about her camera bags, but June assured her that their bags had already been safely stowed inside their assigned roomettes. June sat across from her, fussing with the collar of her cape. She'd donned the thing as soon as they entered the dining car, saying the air conditioning was too cool for her.

"Where are the sleeping cars?" Roi asked.

"They're generally toward the back of the train. The porter will have the rooms made up for us by the time we finish our meal."

Roi studied her. "You do this a lot, don't you?"

"Do what?"

"This." Roi waved a hand to encompass their surroundings. "Travel by train."

"Oh. Yes." June unfolded her napkin and carefully placed it across her lap. "I don't like to fly."

"Why not?"

June looked at her. She seemed surprised by the directness of Roi's question. Before she could reply, their white-coated server arrived to take their drink orders.

Roi asked for a double Crown Manhattan. Up.

June's eyes widened.

"And for the lady?" the server asked.

June consulted her menu. "What are your wine selections tonight?"

The server flipped his notepad open. "Tonight we're featuring a La Crema Chardonnay, a Red Pony Ranch Reserve Pinot Noir, and a Rodney Strong Cabernet."

"I'll have a glass of the Chardonnay, please."

The server nodded and moved on to the next table.

"So. You were saying?"

June gave Roi a small smile. It was almost coquettish. *Almost.* She picked up her water glass. "I don't believe I was saying anything, Mr. Rodgers."

Roi rolled her eyes. "June? Since we're going to be together for most of the next six days, I think there's something we need to clarify."

"What's that?"

Roi leaned forward over their small table and lowered her voice. "I'm not a man. I'm a *woman*."

June in mid-swallow choked on her water. She raised her

napkin to her mouth, but the harder she tried to compose herself, the more she choked.

Heads at other tables swerved toward the distressing sound.

Roi began to stand up, but June waved her back into her seat.

"I'll . . . be . . . fine," she gasped. "I just need a moment."

Roi fidgeted on her seat. What a colossal blunder. Why didn't she wait until . . . when? Hell. There would never have been an easier time.

She looked out the window and was surprised to see that things on the platform were moving. Correction. The platform wasn't moving, *they* were moving. The train was leaving the station—just like she'd left the station with June. There was no going back now. The cat was out of the bag, and it lay stretched out across the tabletop between them, clamoring for attention.

June seemed more composed, although she was still dabbing at her eyes with the end of her napkin.

"Are you okay?" Roi asked.

June nodded.

"I'm sorry I just dropped it on you like that. I guess I thought you'd figure it out."

"Figure it out?"

Roi nodded.

The server arrived and deposited their drinks. "You folks ready to order?"

June didn't reply, so Roi told him they'd need another few minutes. The server didn't seem to notice. He was too busy staring at June, who had picked up her wine glass and proceeded to drain half of its contents in one elegant sequence of energetic swallows.

Roi and the server locked eyes. "Yeah. We're going to need another one of those." She made an oblique gesture toward June's glass.

The server winked and walked off.

Roi waited until June set her near-empty glass back down on the table. "Thirsty?"

June ignored the question. She unclipped the collar of her dark blue cape and slid it off her shoulders. "I don't know why they keep it so warm in here."

Roi opened her mouth to say something, but thought better of it. "You honestly had no idea?" she asked instead.

"No idea about what?" June replied. Her response seemed genuine enough. Roi didn't think she was simply playing dumb.

"No idea that I'm not a man?"

June's face dissolved into another flustered look. Roi quickly extended a hand across the table. "You're not going to choke again, are you?"

She shook her red head.

"I just thought . . . well . . . that somebody at the paper would've told you."

June lifted her chin. "I don't make it a habit to discuss the private lives of my co-workers, Mr.—*Miss* Rodgers."

This was going no place. And it was traveling there a helluva lot faster than the damn Capitol Limited, which appeared to be crawling its way out of Union Station.

Roi sighed. "Please call me Roi."

June didn't reply.

Roi met her blue eyes. "Please?"

"All right. Roi."

There was that maddening little tingle again. She needed to get that shit under control. And fast. She cleared her throat.

"Look. This isn't a thing for you, is it? I mean . . . it won't get in the way of our working relationship, will it?"

"A *thing?*"

Roi sighed. "If you're going to spend the rest of the evening repeating everything I say, this is going to be a very dull conversation."

June actually smiled . . . sort of.

"I apologize. You just took me by surprise. I wasn't expecting . . . that."

Roi crossed her arms. "What *were* you expecting?"

June lowered her gaze and seemed to become absorbed by the blue-and-white pattern on the railway china. Roi gave up and flicked the rim of her empty water glass. The soft *ting* it made was as clear as a bell. June looked up at her.

"Nice stuff." Roi smiled. "You weren't kidding about the first-class accommodations, were you?"

June seemed to relax. A little. She picked up her wine glass again.

"No. The elegance and refinement of train travel is highly underestimated by most people today."

"So I'm beginning to understand."

"Are you making fun of me?"

The question caught Roi off guard. In fact, she *had* been making fun of her. And now, she felt like a schmuck . . . in boi's clothing.

"It's my turn to apologize. I'm sorry for acting like an asshole."

June sighed.

"No," Roi clarified. "I mean it. I'm really sorry. Can we just start over?"

June seemed intrigued by Roi's suggestion. "What does that mean, exactly?"

Roi extended a hand across the table. "Hello. My name is Roisin Rodgers, and I'm a photographer at *The Windy City Mercury*. My friends and family call me Roi for short."

June belatedly took hold of Roi's hand and gave it a modest squeeze. "Roisin? That sounds Irish."

"It is." Roi nodded. "I think it means little rose. It's a family name."

"How interesting. Where are you from?"

"Guess."

"Guess?"

"Sure. You should be able to figure it out."

June thought about it. "Some place in the south?"

Roi smiled at her. "Pretty good. Even though I've tried

hard to lose my accent, I know that it still creeps out. I guess it always will."

June seemed fascinated. "Where in the south?"

"North Carolina. Asheville."

"Asheville? Where the Biltmore Estate is?"

"Have you been there?"

June shook her head. "No, but I've always longed to go—ever since I read *Look Homeward Angel*."

"Ah. Well the reality is a lot more imposing, and a lot less poetic. And it costs almost as much to get in as it does to get out."

"I'm not sure I know what you mean."

"Suffice it to say that I didn't have the greatest experience growing up there."

"I'm sorry to hear that."

June sounded like she meant it. Roi decided it was safer not to wander any further down this path. At least for tonight.

"So." Roi sipped at her own drink. It was a bold combination of bitter and sweet. "Tell me about yourself. Where are you from? I mean, tell me the things that aren't in your official bio."

"Oh. That's easy. I grew up in Wisconsin. Dairyland."

"Where in Wisconsin?"

June smiled. "In *Dairyland*. That's the actual name of the town."

"Seriously? There's actually a place called Dairyland?"

"Oh, yes. In fact, the town slogan is 'Dairyland: Wisconsin's Dairyland.' You'll find it at the intersection of Wisconsin Highway Thirty-Five and County Road T." She chuckled. "Things are simpler in the heartland."

No kidding.

Roi was captivated. "Brothers and sisters?"

"Two brothers. Twins. Marty and Mattie."

Marty and Mattie?

"Really? Are they older or younger?"

"Younger." June smiled. "They both stayed on in Dairyland. They help our father run the family farm."

Of course they do.

"How about you?" June was leaning forward now. "Any brothers or sisters?"

Roi sighed. "One brother. When he isn't cooling his heels in the Buncombe County jail, he stays active by moving his meth lab to new and improved locations along the French Broad River."

June blinked. "Oh, dear. I'm sorry to hear that."

"Don't be." Roi shrugged. "We just chose different ways to escape."

Their stalwart server arrived with June's second glass of Chardonnay. He set it down and regarded Roi with a raised eyebrow.

"I guess we'd better order some food," Roi said to June.

"Would you like to order for us?" June asked, demurely.

"Um. Sure." Roi was surprised, but she snapped up the menu and looked it over. The fare wasn't terribly exotic, but it all sounded decent. She guessed that June probably wasn't much of a meat eater, even though she hailed from a part of the country where men were men, and sheep were scared. "I'll have the Amtrak Signature Steak, medium rare. And the lady will have the roasted chicken with the rice and vegetable medley."

"Yes, sir," the server said. "We'll have that right up for you."

When he departed, Roi sighed and looked at June apologetically. "I get that a lot."

"I'm relieved to know that I'm not the only one who made that mistake."

Roi smiled. "Not by a long shot."

June was rotating the stem of her wine glass back and forth between her long fingers. "So why do you do it?"

"Do what?"

"You know." June gave a mild shrug that was more like flinch. "Dress . . . in that . . . *confusing* fashion?"

"I told you. I'm a boi. It's what we do."

"Boy? I don't understand."

"Not 'boy,' as in b-o-y. 'Boi,' as in b-o-i. Meaning I'm biologically a woman, but I prefer to present myself as androgynous." She took another sip of her drink. "You're in a medical profession. You must have some familiarity with the concept?"

"Of course." June was still twisting her wine glass. "I've just never had any direct . . . interactions . . . with a practitioner."

Practitioner?

Roi smiled. "I have to say that I've been called a lot of things in my day, but 'practitioner' is one for the record books."

June blushed. "I didn't mean to offend you."

"Oh, god." Roi extended a hand toward June. "I'm *not* offended. I didn't mean it like that." She shook her head. "I grew up being called names like skank, fag, queer, pervert, and bulldyke—and that was just at home." She smiled. "Believe me when I tell you that being called a practitioner is like getting a promotion. I regard it as a compliment."

June looked relieved. "I'm glad. I feel like a fish out of water sometimes."

Roi didn't trust herself to comment.

"Why did they call you queer?" June asked. Her voice was so low that Roi barely heard the question.

"I suppose because I am."

June looked confused.

"Queer," Roi clarified. "I'm a lesbian."

June's wine glass lurched to the side. Roi reached out and caught it before it toppled over.

"I guess I need to parcel these revelations out."

June's clumsiness made it clear to Roi that her mortification was increasing.

"I don't know what's gotten into me," she explained. "You must think I'm a complete klutz."

In fact, Roi wasn't at all sure *what* she thought June might be, but klutz wasn't on the list of possibilities. She said as much, but June just shook the observation off.

"You're just being kind."

"Not really . . ."

June met Roi's eyes. They gazed at each other across the modest gulf of table until the quiet between them merged with the subliminal clack-clack, clack-clack, clack-clack of the train wheels, gliding along the silver rails beneath them.

No. Roi didn't think June was a klutz. Klutz had no place in the universe of adjectives that suddenly spread out in front of her. All manner of minor key vibrations were now banging away inside her, foretelling dire prognostications of certain catastrophe. She was on the brink of deciding that she didn't care, and was about ready to say as much when a rolling cart screeched to a halt beside their table.

Fortunately for both of them, their salads had arrived. By unspoken, mutual consent, they embraced the happy diversion and spent the rest of their time in the dining car making light conversation about the differences that separated land from air travel.

For Roi, the solace of privacy in the confines of her bedtime roomette couldn't come soon enough.

"BUT THERE MUST be some mistake . . ."

June repeated the same phrase half-a-dozen times to the beleaguered porter, who tried again to explain that their reservation was for *one* roomette.

She felt herself starting to panic. This could not be happening. Not now. Not after the revelations in the dining car.

She closed her eyes and quickly ran through the steps to avoid panic attacks that were outlined in her trusty Merck Manual.

Reduce anxiety to decrease tension and lower the amount of stress in your life. Impossible right now.

Perform relaxation exercises. Engage in ten to twenty minutes of deep breathing. A physical and logistical impossibility within the next ninety seconds.

Get your heart rate up through regular physical exercise. Short of running several laps through a half-mile of rail cars, this would not help much right now.

Limit your intake of alcohol. Too late for that one.

Change your thinking about a problem or situation. Bingo.

Her eyes flew open. *I just need to change my approach to the situation. I have no reason to feel anxious. Impropriety isn't a factor because Roi isn't a man. Roi is a woman.*

Roi is a woman.

June swayed into the wall of narrow corridor.

The porter reached out a hand to steady her. "You okay, miss?"

"I'm fine," June assured him. "The train must have jolted me off my footing."

"There's a lot of that going on," a low voice behind her commented. It was Roi. She'd been off getting background photos of the sleeper cars, and some views of the nighttime landscape that surrounded the train. June was surprised that she was back from her errand so soon.

She turned to face her and felt her queasiness return.

Roi appeared to notice her distress.

"June." Roi's tone was placating. "It's really okay. It's only for a few hours, and we'll both sleep right through it." She glanced at her watch. "And at the crack of four, we have to be up to make our transfer in Pittsburgh."

"But Max—"

"I just talked with Max."

June was surprised. "You did? What did he say?"

"Before or after he told me to shove this train up my chocolate whiz-wang?"

The porter snickered.

June blushed up to the roots of her hair.

"Yeah. It looks like we just have to make the best of it." Roi smiled at June and slapped her palm against the doorway to their roomette—which really resembled a set of bunk beds, stuffed inside a tin can. "So. Are you a top or a bottom?"

The porter snorted.

Roi glared at him. "I think we've got this...you probably have other fish to fry."

"Yes, sir." The porter touched the brim of his cap and hurried away. Before exiting the car, he turned around. "You just let us know if there's anything we can do to make your experience more . . . enjoyable."

"Right." Roi waved at him. "Thanks. I think we have everything we need."

The porter looked June up and down. "Yes, sir, I think you do, too."

Roi took a step forward, but June caught hold of her arm.

"It's fine," she said. She addressed the porter. "Thank you for your help."

The porter disappeared behind the door that connected their car to the next sleeper in line.

"What an asshole."

June looked at Roi. "He's just doing his job."

"Not that part," Roi explained. "He could stuff the commentary."

"I don't blame him. I did overreact."

"Well. Don't worry about it. Max is a cheap bastard. We should've expected this."

June chose not to comment on that.

"So." Roi pointed down the narrow corridor toward the opposite end of the car. "I passed the lavatory back there. Judging by the size of this roomette, I'm thinking it will be a better place to change."

June agreed. "You're probably right."

"How about we divide and conquer?" Roi reached over to the luggage rack that sat across from their roomette and grabbed her backpack. "You can change in the bathroom down here, and I'll go upstairs and change in another one."

June nodded her assent, and Roi took off toward the stairway that led to the upper level of their sleeping car. June continued to stand in the center of the narrow corridor for a few moments, shooting nervous looks back and forth between the neatly made-up berths in their cubby hole, and the nearest escape route. She wondered how fast the train was traveling, and how likely it would be that she'd sustain serious injury if she jumped off? They'd be rolling into Fort Wayne soon, and the Lutheran hospital there was a Level II trauma center . . .

Ridiculous. She shook her head. They were both adults. This would be no different than sharing a room with Letty. After all, Letty was a lesbian, and June never felt uncomfortable around her—except when Letty teased her about . . . things.

She squared her shoulders and picked up her train case. If she hurried, she could be safely in bed and under the covers before Roi returned.

ROI NORMALLY SLEPT in the buff, but that wasn't happening on this trip—not when she had to make the walk of shame back to their sleeping quarters. So she compromised and pulled on a loose-fitting tank top and pair of boxer shorts. They'd just have to suffice. It was only for one night, after all. And it wasn't like she had to worry about Nurse Goody getting any amorous ideas.

God. June had been like a deer in the headlights when Roi had told her she was a woman.

She bent over the sink and looked at herself in the tiny mirror.

I don't look that much like a guy. Not really.

She turned her face to the side and examined the lines of her short haircut.

Well. Maybe I look like a guy a little bit . . .

She slowly rotated her head from side to side. *But not in a scary, butch way.*

Someone tapped at the door to the bathroom. Again.

"Just a second," she called out. "I'm nearly finished."

She sighed and glared at herself. *What the hell is the matter with you?*

She looked at her watch. They only had seven hours to endure this torture. Then they'd be up at the butt crack of dawn to make their transfer in Pittsburgh. And after that?

Eight more hours on another tin can before they reached Philadelphia.

Well. She collected her toiletries and stuffed them back into her backpack. *Nobody can say I'm not a team player.*

She opened the door and squeezed past the very large, impatient man waiting outside in the corridor. He was all but hanging onto his crotch. She thought she recognized him from the dining car . . . he was the one who sat at the table across from them and kept staring at June.

It was hard to blame him for that. It was pretty hard not to stare at her.

She lucked out and didn't run into anyone else on her way back downstairs.

The door to their roomette was closed, and the black interior curtain was pulled across its window. Roi stashed her backpack in their luggage compartment and tapped softly on the door.

"June? Are you in there?"

She heard something like a scuffling sound. The latch on the door slid back. Then there were more scuffling noises.

"Yes. You can come in."

Roi opened the door. The lights were turned off, but there was enough ambient light seeping in from the corridor to allow her to recognize the outlines of a nurse-shaped bundle beneath the covers on the lower bunk. She stepped inside and slid the door closed behind her. It was pitch black. She was wedged

*"Don't worry," Roi said with a conspiratorial smile.
"I'll keep your dirty little secret."*

into about ten inches of space and her knees were touching the edge of the lower berth.

"So, I guess I'm on top?" she asked the dark bundle.

"Is that okay with you?" June's voice sounded small and distant.

"Sure. Just tell me how I get up there."

"There are some steps built in along the wall to your left."

"I don't suppose you'd consider turning on a light?"

It took June a few seconds to reply. "I'd really prefer not to, if you don't mind."

"Right." Roi sighed. "Okay. Here goes."

She turned to the left and took a blind step forward. The steps weren't along the wall, they were dead ahead. Her shin slammed into the center of the lower tread.

"God *fucking* damn it!" She bent over and grabbed her leg.

"What happened?" June asked in an anxious voice.

Roi was still bent over. Lightning sharp bolts of pain were shooting up her leg.

"I hit my damn leg on the bottom stair."

Roi could hear June sitting up. "Are you all right?"

Roi was tempted to ask June if she fucking sounded all right—but bit back the expletive.

"I'm so sorry." June's voice sounded a lot closer now. "I should've turned the light on for you."

Roi couldn't tell if the pain in her leg was starting to recede, or if the sudden scent of ginger that was filling up her senses was just making her forget about how much it hurt. She pivoted toward the wonderful smell and straightened up from her crouch.

Bad idea.

Her head connected with the underside of the top bunk. Hard. She went down like a ton of bricks.

June snapped on a reading light in time to see her collapse into the tiny bit of floor space that separated the lower bunk from the interior wall of the roomette.

"Oh, my goodness." June pushed her covers back and scrambled across the berth. "Are you all right?"

Roi was holding her head between her hands. "No."

"Come up here." June took hold of Roi's arm and tugged her up onto the bunk to sit beside her. Roi was still clutching her head, but June gently moved her hands away. "Let me take a look."

Roi's instinct was to pull away from her, but she didn't. June's hands were soft and warm. They cupped her face and lowered her head so she could examine the affected area. Roi felt her fingertips softly gliding over the bump that was already rising up on the side of her forehead.

"Does this hurt?" she asked.

Roi swallowed. June was wearing a low-cut white night-gown, and it clung to every perfect part of her. Right now, *nothing* hurt. In fact, everything was beginning to feel just *fine.*

June said something else, but Roi was having trouble understanding her. The view in front of her was just too mesmerizing. June's ample chest was rising and falling in perfect syncopation with the blood that was now pounding its way along all of Roi's extremities.

She belatedly raised her head to apologize, and to ask June to repeat her question.

Big mistake.

June's face was only inches away from hers, and in the dim light, her blue eyes glowed like sapphires.

Jesus. The woman was fucking gorgeous.

June still had a hand cupping the side of her face, and Roi leaned into her palm. The not-so-subtle rocking of the train was a perfect complement to her own tangled maze of emotions.

June opened her mouth to say something else, but Roi just shook her head. It was pointless. She couldn't hear anything but the hammering of her heart.

The train seemed to lurch and they swayed toward each other on the narrow bunk.

But something else was happening. The train was slowing down.

Yellow-and-white lights began to flash around the edges of the black window curtain.

The train whistle sounded. Once. Twice. Then two shorter blasts.

June blinked and seemed to collect herself. She dropped her hand and sat back.

"This must be Fort Wayne." Her voice was husky.

Roi was still in a fog. "Indiana?"

June nodded.

"We're stopping?"

June nodded again. She discreetly took hold of a pillow and tugged it over so she could hold it against her chest. "Do you want to get some ice for your head?"

Roi raised her hand to her forehead and rubbed her temple. "No. I think I'll be okay." She glanced at the offending set of steps. "I think I'll take advantage of the light and climb up into bed."

"Good idea." June nodded. "I'm so sorry about all of this."

Roi gave her a small smile. "It's okay." She got to her feet, and her foot knocked something over. She heard the dull sounds of small somethings rolling out across the floor.

"Oh, man." Roi bent down and retrieved an open, yellow-and-brown box. "I must've knocked this over when I went down." She gave the small carton a modest shake. "It sounds like most them fell out."

June looked stricken and hastily grabbed the offending item out of Roi's hands.

"Don't worry," Roi said with a conspiratorial smile. "I'll keep your dirty little secret."

June looked up at her in horror.

"Relax. It's not a sin." Roi winked at her and climbed up the steps to her bunk. "I like Milk Duds, too."

CHAPTER THREE
Wake Me Up Before You Go-Go

INCREDIBLY, THEIR TRANSFER in Pittsburgh happened right on schedule. By six-thirty a.m., they'd had breakfast and were nicely settled in big, comfortable seats in the train's observation car. Roi had already shot several dozen pre-dawn photos of June greeting a cadre of fans who had somehow managed to recognize her as they strolled beneath the great dome of Pittsburgh's Union Station. June continued to be amazed at how people could pick her out of a crowd—even when she wasn't wearing her "nurse outfit," as Max called it.

As it happened, June was not wearing her customary, white uniform today. Instead, she'd opted for one of her smart traveling suits. This one was pale green, and she liked the way the close fitting cut of the suit made her feel. It was both professional and casual, all at the same time. And today, she needed all the help she could muster to feel professional.

Roi was dozing on the seat beside her. June didn't blame her at all. She knew that *she'd* certainly got little sleep last night—especially after their disturbing encounter when Roi entered the roomette.

June was mortified by her response to the situation. She'd behaved like an awkward adolescent. It was insupportable. What was the matter with her? It was most unprofessional. And it wasn't like anything inappropriate *could* happen. After all Roi was a woman.

Roi was a woman.

She forced herself to push that thought aside. She resolved to concentrate on her book.

It was a mystery novel Letty had lent her for the trip. Letty knew that June enjoyed mysteries.

"Trust me, honey," Letty said as she shoved the paperback into June's hands. "This one's got your name all over it."

June lowered her eyes and began to reread the page.

> Jane was certainly taking her time. Cordelia stood, attempting to see if anyone was stirring over near the bridge. Sitting back down, she let her mind stray to warm scones and hot tea with lemon waiting for her at The Lyme House . . .

Roi had looked so helpless when June had turned on her reading light and saw her, wedged between the bunk and the door to their roomette, holding her head between her hands.

> "Something's wrong, isn't it?" asked Cordelia. "Ever since we sat down here I've felt it."

June had felt something, too. And it wasn't a *normal* something. It certainly wasn't anything she could find a reference for in her Merck Manual.

> "We've got to call the police. I found a body under the bridge. It's a young woman. I'm afraid she's dead."

Roi was young, too. Far younger than June. And Roi was a woman.

Roi was a woman.

She shook her head. This was getting her no place.

> "It took me a minute to find the dogs. I suppose they went under the bridge as soon as they caught the scent. She was facedown in the water by the shore. I pulled her out and laid her by the bank." Jane paused. The stillness in the air made her words sound unnaturally

loud. "I know her. She belongs to the sorority. Her name's Allison Lord." For some reason she found it important to say the name out loud. A kind of benediction perhaps.

It was important to say the name out loud.

She'd always believed that, too.

How many times had she given that advice to patients or their distressed family members? It was one of the first principles of emotional healing. Name your demons: because in so doing, you deprive them of their power. It was one of the basic tenets of every twelve-step program. And it worked for a reason.

Did she have demons?

If so, they were unknown to her. And that fact rendered her powerless to name them. The prospect of doing so was simply too frightening.

Roi stirred on the seat beside her, unfolded her legs, and attempted to re-cross them, but the effort caused her to wince.

It must be the bruise from hitting her shin on the stair tread.

June chastised herself again for her failure to examine Roi's leg. It was a complete breach of competence on her part. The truth was, she'd been wholly distracted by the sensation of running her fingertips over Roi's smooth forehead. She'd been saved from any further lapses of protocol by their arrival at the terminal in Fort Wayne.

The view from the observation car was breathtaking. The train was skirting the edges of the Juniata River again. She could see water glinting just behind the trees that hemmed the steep railroad grade. They'd pretty much been following the tributary ever since they had left Pittsburgh. It looked wider and more imposing now—probably suggesting that they were getting close to its union with the great Susquehanna. That meant they were not far from Harrisburg.

The entire trip across the Keystone State had been visually stunning. The route *The Pennsylvanian* traveled wound them in and around multiple ridges of the densely forested Allegheny Mountains and a bevy of ancient water gaps. Soon they would be crossing the rich farmlands of Lancaster County and arriving at the 30th Street Station in Philadelphia. Then this part of the journey would be over.

She fervently hoped that the remainder of their trip would be less . . . confounding.

"You certainly look lost in thought."

The voice startled her and she dropped her book.

Roi reached out a hand and caught it before it hit the floor. "Sorry." She handed the novel back to June. "I didn't mean to scare you."

"Don't apologize." June tried to conceal how flustered she felt. "I was mesmerized by the view."

"It is pretty beautiful. I've been enjoying it."

"I thought you were asleep?"

"Dozing off and on." Roi yawned. "I've never been able to sleep sitting up."

"I'm afraid you didn't get much rest last night."

Roi smiled at her. "Likewise."

June lowered her eyes.

Roi touched her gently on the forearm. "I don't mean to be so cavalier. I know that last night was difficult for you."

June felt her panic returning. "What do you mean?"

"Having to share that tin can-sized room." Roi shrugged. "It was contemptible. I always knew Max was a cheap bastard, but that was pretty extreme—even for him."

"Oh. Max. He can be trying, sometimes."

"Sometimes?" Roi raised an eyebrow. "Why do you put up with the ridiculous amount of travel he saddles you with?"

"I don't really mind, as long as the trips don't conflict with my teaching schedule at the hospital."

Roi looked at her with interest. "I don't know much about that part of your work. What do you teach, exactly?"

"I'm an adjunct member of the faculty in the nursing school at Rush. I teach classes in adult health and gerontology. I also serve as a clinical supervisor to junior and senior students in the medical surgery unit."

"Really?" Roi seemed intrigued. "What does that entail?"

"It's the first opportunity for student nurses to practice things like IM injections, dispensing medications, inserting Foley catheters, performing bed baths—as well as teaching patients how to manage activities of daily living."

"What's an IM injection?"

June smiled. "Intra muscular."

Roi made a face.

"It's not that bad," June assured her. "Not if you do it correctly."

"I suppose you'd say the same thing about bed baths?"

"Well . . ."

"I thought so."

June didn't make any reply. It didn't seem like a safe topic.

Roi was studying her and chewing the inside of her cheek. She had a mischievous expression on her face.

Against her better judgment, June took the bait. "What is it?"

"I was just thinking that I bet you get a lot of requests to demonstrate your technique."

June blushed. "I wouldn't say that . . ."

"Well, I bet you'll be able to after *this* weekend." Roi chuckled.

June didn't reply.

Roi noticed that people around them were starting to collect their belongings and pack up their laptop computers. "What's up?" she asked June. "Are we stopping again?"

June nodded. "We're probably coming into Harrisburg."

"Oh, really?" Roi stood up, too. "I think I'll try to get some pictures."

"Good idea. It should be beautiful when the two rivers come together."

Roi didn't disagree with her. "Wanna come with me?"

"Where are you going?"

"The back of the train. The best views are from the last car."

June considered that. Maybe it was true. Things were a lot clearer when you were looking back at them. That probably was because they were already in the past and you didn't have to worry so much about what lay ahead.

She decided that right now, a view like that appealed to her. She took hold of her bag and got to her feet.

"Lead on," she said to Roi. "I'm right behind you."

THE TRAVELERS IN Philadelphia's 30th Street Station were scurrying around like ants. Red ants. *Bad-tempered red ants.*

June didn't understand why they were all so . . . cranky. They pushed and surged and wove in and out around them as if they were standing still. True, they were moving somewhat slowly through the big, central terminal. But that was only because they were looking for the appropriate street exit to meet their car and driver.

"Over there." Roi pointed toward the 29th Street exit. "That's where the pedestrian drop-off and pick-up areas are located."

She took hold of June's arm and guided her past the massive Angel of the Resurrection statue that dominated the concourse.

They stepped outside, and June was surprised by how warm it was. The temperature in Chicago had been hovering in the lower fifties. But it had to be nearly seventy degrees here. People were walking around in shorts and t-shirts. She now regretted her wardrobe choice.

"It should be perfect weather at the beach." Roi stopped and set down her camera bags. She took off her lightweight leather jacket and folded it over the top of her roller bag. June wished she could do the same, but unfortunately, she wasn't wearing anything beneath the tailored jacket to her suit.

There was a light breeze blowing, and it stirred the hair that fell across Roi's forehead. June could see traces of a bruise forming there.

She felt another surge of guilt.

Roi was looking around at the myriad of taxis and private cars that were lined up outside the station entrance. Drivers were holding up white placards displaying names printed in bold, block letters.

Schumacher. Feldstein. Arnold. Fink. Newmann.

No Magee. No Rodgers. No *Windy City Mercury*.

"Do you see anything?" Roi asked June.

She shook her head. "No."

"I feel like we've stumbled into an accountant's convention."

June looked at her, and Roi gave her a shrug and a smile.

"How about that one?" June thought she saw a flash of something promising.

"Acme Instrument Company?" Roi asked.

"Oh. I guess not."

Roi chuckled.

"Maybe we should try calling the CAMP Rehoboth number?" June was digging around inside her handbag. "Dorrie gave it to me as a backup."

Roi touched her elbow. "Wait a minute. Look over there."

"Where?" June didn't see anything.

Roi took hold of her shoulders and turned her around. "*There*. See that . . . guy . . . leaning against the front of the hoopty?"

June looked at Roi. "What on earth is a hoopty?"

"It's a big, gas-guzzling car. Like that one, right *there*."

June finally saw what Roi was referring to. It looked like a relic from her father's time. Sleek. Bright red. And half-a-block long. It was parked somewhat askew behind a line of taxis. An oddly dressed person was propped-up against the impressive grill of the car and holding what appeared to be an iPad.

She squinted. "What is that on the screen?"

Roi started laughing. "I think it's Jackie Zeman."

June was confused. "Who on earth is Jackie Zeman?"

"You're kidding me, right?"

"No." June looked at Roi. "Should I know who that is?"

"Come on." Roi took hold of her arm again. "I think our ride is here."

When they got closer to the big, red car, June could clearly see that the image on the iPad was a nurse. Or at least, it was a redheaded woman *dressed* like a nurse.

"Is that supposed to be me?" she whispered to Roi.

"No. It's an actress who played a nurse on TV. *General Hospital.*"

"The soap opera?"

Roi nodded.

"How strange." June was staring at their driver. He certainly was . . . *eclectic*. "I wonder why he did that?"

The man in question finally seemed to notice them. He stood up straight and pulled his oversized aviator sunglasses down the bridge of his nose. Then he waved at them with dramatic flourishes.

"Is you the famous nurse?" he gushed as they approached. June couldn't pinpoint his thick, Hispanic accent. South American, perhaps? He was outrageously attired in hot pants, flip-flops, and a cropped, black mesh tank top.

And he was still jabbering with excitement. "Oh, *girl* . . . I see you brung along a fresh boi toy." He was giving Roi a good once-over. "Honey . . . you gonna be more popular than chicken legs in a crab cage."

June was speechless.

Roi stepped into the void. "This is June Magee, R.N. We're from the *Windy City Mercury*. Are you the driver from CAMP Rehoboth?"

"Driver? *Hel-lo?* You see these legs?" He snapped his fingers. "No, cariño. I dances at The Blue Lagoon. Miz Bonnie call me from the golf course and ax me to fetch you cause Miz

Fay got all MIXX'd up." He chuckled. "Third time this week."
He waved a manicured hand toward the big Delta 88. "Hop in,
hop in. I'm late for an appointment."

Roi seemed to be deliberating. "I'm not sure . . ."

June laid a hand on her arm.

"What is your name?" she asked their . . . dancer.

"Pico." He smiled broadly. "Pico de Gallo. At your service."

"Pico de gallo?" Roi repeated.

"Is a stage name . . . you know? Just like Ru Paul or Carol
Channing."

June was confused. "I don't think Carol Channing had a
stage name . . ."

Pico had already moved on. He was walking around the
massive car toward the trunk. "Come on, come on. *Vamanos.*
We need to roll."

Roi sighed and carried their bags to rear of the vehicle.

June noticed something on the ground near the front tire. It
looked like an oversized drink cup—but it was full of money.
Dollar bills. Lots of them. She picked it up.

"Oh, Mr. de Gallo?" she held up the cup. "Is this yours?"

"Ay ay. *Sí, cariño.*" Pico slapped a hand against his forehead. "That's my Big Gulp. I uses it for tips." He smacked Roi
on the shoulder. "You was takin' so long I decided to make
some hays while the sun was out . . . you know?"

"Right. Of *course* you did." Roi loaded their last bag into
the trunk and Pico slammed the enormous lid closed.

"Come, on. Come on. Get insides." Pico hurried forward
and opened the back door to the car. "Just push that trash off
the seats. I got some foods on my way up here."

June handed him the cup full of cash and climbed in. She
slid across the big bench seat and collected several wrinkled
wads of yellow paper. *Fried Bologna and Velveeta Biscuit*
was printed across the wrappers in bright orange letters. She
dropped them to the floorboard like they were on fire. Roi got
in after her and the two of them settled into the plush backseat
that was roughly the size of a sofa.

Pico de Gallo

Pico slid into the front seat and started the car. The big machine shuddered to life and strains from "If I Can't Have You" blasted out of the radio at ear-splitting volume. The disco tune was plainly one of Pico's favorites. He was already rocking like a metronome at prestissimo.

"Could you turn that down, please?" Roi shouted.

Pico didn't seem to hear her.

Roi slid forward to the edge of the seat to repeat her request just as Pico executed an abrupt, full-throttle U-turn. Brakes screeched and horns blared all around them. Roi was hurled across the backseat and ended up face down, half sprawled across June's lap.

Pico saw them in his rearview mirror and hollered above the din. "Can you tortilleras waits until we leaves the station before you gets busy?"

June was stunned as she stared down at her lap full of Roi.

The sensation, although unexpected, was not unpleasant. She had to resist the temptation to reach out and touch Roi's thick, dark hair.

Roi quickly pushed herself up so her face wasn't smashed into June's lap. Of course that brought her eyes level with the buttons on June's bodice—a position that didn't decrease June's agitation. Roi hovered there for a few moments, suspended on her forearms, while the car continued to careen away from the station. She sat up and attempted to compose herself once it was clear that the car was safely headed in a consistently straight direction.

Yvonne Elliman was still crooning at decibel ranges that were certain to cause permanent hearing loss. The Oldsmobile was now gliding along the Schuylkill Expressway toward I-95. Roi decided to try again. She leaned forward and tapped Pico on the shoulder.

"Would you *please* turn down the music?" she bellowed.

"Ay ay, you don't have to shout." Pico reached out to the radio dial and lowered the volume.

Roi sat back gave June a forlorn look.

They were on the interstate now. Heading south. The traffic was moving well, even though several of the lanes were closed for construction. The road appeared to have more potholes than pavement, but Pico didn't seem to mind. He just floored the accelerator and kept surging ahead.

Roi and June were getting bounced around on the big backseat like a couple of Ping-Pong balls. June worried that her foundation garment was not equal to the task of keeping her endowments in check. She did her best to keep her arms pressed tightly against her sides, but it was a losing battle.

"How long until we reach Rehoboth Beach?" she asked Pico.

He waved a hand at her. June noticed that he had French tips on his nails. "Is a good two hours—but I needs to make a stop first."

"A stop?" Roi didn't sound happy about that. "Where?"

"Is just up here. Not far. In Chester."

"Chester?" Roi shot June an anxious look, then faced Pico again. "I don't think that's a good idea."

"Is fine. Ten minute. You stays in the car."

Roi didn't appear to be satisfied with that response. She began to argue with Pico, but he chose that instant to charge across four lanes of traffic and veer onto an exit ramp. Roi and June were hurled into each other again. June gave up on trying to preserve any modicum of modesty. It was taking all the agility she could muster just to remain upright on the backseat.

Pico was flying down the exit ramp at light speed. There was a stoplight at the bottom, but he ignored it and made a sharp left turn onto a boulevard that cut through a swath of boarded-up row houses and empty retail storefronts.

"Where the hell are we going?" Roi didn't sound very happy.

Pico didn't answer. He was busy blowing his horn at a jaywalking pedestrian who was moving too slowly to suit him. The hunched-over man was standing in the middle of the street, drinking from an oversized aluminum can. He was carrying a white plastic bag that appeared to contain more of the same beverage.

June was mesmerized by the spectacle. It reminded her of a PBS documentary she'd once seen about urban decline in the cities of America's rust belt.

But the big Delta 88 was rolling again. They were surging up Kerlin Street past block after block of condemned buildings, vacant lots, and gas stations that no longer had functioning pumps.

The only business that seemed to be thriving in Chester was the one that sold plywood. June had never seen so much of it in one place. She was about to comment on that when Pico made another sharp turn and they screeched to a halt in the parking lot of a shopworn Sunoco station. Unlike the majority of other businesses in town, this one appeared to be doing a brisk business. Cars were lined up on both sides of its two working gas pumps. Pico cut the engine and turned around on his seat to face them.

"Okay. I gotta runs inside. But you two stays in the car—and don't give no money to any of these putas."

June looked enquiringly at Roi, who held up a hand.

"Don't ask," she said.

Pico opened his door and was immediately set upon by half-a-dozen vagrants, all begging for handouts. He waved them all off and left them in his fabulous wake as he flip-flopped his way across the parking lot to enter the tiny store.

"I've got a bad feeling about this." Roi shifted closer to June on the seat. It seemed like a protective maneuver.

"What do you mean?"

"I don't think our go-go boy can be up to anything good here."

"Go-go boy?" June was confused.

"Yeah. Pico. The 'dancer.'" Roi made air quotes around the word.

"You don't think he's really a dancer?" June asked.

"Oh, no. He's a dancer all right. It's the rest of this little errand that has me worried."

June touched Roi on the knee, but immediately withdrew her hand. She'd intended it to be a simple, placating gesture— but for some reason, it felt intimate.

"I wouldn't worry," she said quickly to cover her embarrassment. "He seems like a sweet boy."

"Right." Roi was peering out the window. "Here comes our sweet boy now. And just what the hell does he have?"

Pico was making his way back to the car, and he was carrying three large cardboard boxes. He sat them down on the hood and opened the front passenger door.

"I needs you to take one of these back there," he said after he'd stashed two of the boxes up front.

'Of course." June opened her door and prepared to step out, but Pico stopped her.

"No, no, *cariño*." He waved her back. "Stays inside. Just slides that tight tushie over."

June did as she was told and Pico placed the third box on the seat beside her. He slammed the door and walked back around the car to climb in behind the wheel.

"See?" He said to Roi. "Not even ten minute. Just like I tell you."

He started the car and backed up without looking behind them. Horns blared.

"Watch where the fuck you're going, you fuck-stick fag!"

Roi and June exchanged nervous glances. Pico gunned the engine and burned rubber as he left the parking lot and made an illegal turn back onto Kerlin Street.

Roi took hold of June's hand. June didn't complain.

They were barreling back up the road toward the interstate, but June noticed there were no signs for southbound on-ramps.

"I don't think we can get back on the highway this way," she offered.

Pico waved her off. "Is okay. I knows a shortcut."

He turned off the main road and cut through a series of

one-way streets that were lined with houses that had once been fine, but now were worn down from years of neglect. Each block they passed seemed bleaker and more dilapidated than the previous one. It was like watching the spread of an infectious disease—something June knew a lot about.

The street they were traveling t-boned into another main thoroughfare. Pico took a left, then an immediate sharp right and bounced the big car up and over the curb to roar across a vacant stretch of land that was dotted with uncut patches of tall grass.

"Where the hell are you going?" Roi sounded alarmed, and she wasn't trying to conceal her agitation.

"To the highway, chica. This the shortcut I tell you about."

"The highway?" They were still bouncing along the uneven ground. "This isn't even a damn road!"

The terrain around them was littered with cast-off car parts, empty beer cans, and a couple of old mattresses that were covered with suspicious-looking stains. There was even something that looked uncannily like half of a parade float.

Pico cut the wheel hard to the left and the car bounced down over a concealed curb and onto another stretch of potholed pavement. The abrupt change in direction sent everything inside the car flying. This time, June ended up sprawled across Roi, and the box that Pico had deposited on the backseat fell off, spilling its contents across the floorboards.

Roi helped June back to a sitting position.

"What the hell is the matter with you?" she yelled at Pico. "You're driving like a damn lunatic."

"Will you relax and looks around? Is the highway—just like I tell you."

Sure enough, they were merging back on to I-95.

June could tell that Roi was on the verge of either strangling Pico, or insisting that he pull off at the next exit so they could get out of his car. She decided to try and defuse the situation.

"Will you help me pick these things up?" she asked Roi.

The floorboards were covered with hundreds of brightly

colored rings. Purple. Red. Bright blue. Lime green. Even fuchsia. June collected an assortment of them and looped them over the fingers of her left hand.

"These are really lovely," she commented.

Roi watched her impassively for a moment. Then her expression changed.

"June . . ." she began.

"What are these things, Mr. de Gallo?" June asked. She held her hand up so he could see the multicolored display.

"June . . ." Roi tried again.

June was rotating her hand back and forth, watching the light play across the ornaments that festooned her long fingers.

"They're so bright and cheery. Are they key rings?"

Roi raised a hand to her forehead.

Pico saw what June was holding and began to cackle.

"*Sí, cariño*—they's rings all right. But they don't unlock no doors." He continued to guffaw. "Except maybe *back* doors, if you knows what I mean."

"Back doors?" June looked confused.

"Yoo hoo, boi?" Pico looked at Roi in the rearview mirror. "You wanna splain to your nurse what kinds of rings these is?"

Roi glared at him. "No. I really don't."

"Why? Is you scared?"

June was looking back and forth between the two of them. "What am I missing?"

"Not much, *cariño*," Pico explained. "You just found my box of swag."

"Swag?"

"*Sí. Blue Lagoon swag*. For the bar. Is what I pick up from Alphonse in Chester. He knows how to get *anything*."

June was still adding rings to her fingers. "They're all different sizes."

Pico snorted. "You got that part right, nurse."

Roi took hold of June's hand and lowered it to the seat.

"Let's just put these back into the box, okay?"

June met Roi's eyes. Enlightenment began to dawn.

"These aren't key rings, are they?"

Roi shook her head.

June looked down at her hand. Then back at Roi. Her eyes grew wide.

"Oh, my *god* . . ."

Roi carefully pulled the rings off June's fingers and dropped them back into the box.

Pico was still laughing. "Is okay, nurse. They ain't been used, yet."

Roi glared at him. "Just drive the car, okay?"

"Okay. But I thing you should keep a few for yourself."

June was mortified. "Why ever would we do that?"

"Cause you never know when your boi gonna need help stayin' up all night."

June was speechless. She dropped her gaze, but all she could see was a sea of tiny, Technicolor cock rings.

Roi sighed. "Pico?"

"*Sí,* bepi?"

Roi sat back and extended an arm out along the back of the seat behind June's shoulders.

"Turn up the music."

CHAPTER FOUR
Beyond the Sea

THE ATLANTIC SANDS Hotel had presided over the boardwalk in Rehoboth Beach since 1959—and that appeared to be one of its greatest claims to fame. Leave it to Max to book them in what was arguably one of the oldest inns in town.

Not that it was without appeal. The Sands exuded lots of old-world, beachy charm. It reminded Roi of one of those hotels that figured so prominently in '60s era movies like *Where the Boys Are*. It wouldn't surprise her in the least to round a corner and see George Hamilton or Dolores Hart sunning on striped towels near the cement pool.

No. Not Dolores Hart. She ended up leaving Hollywood and becoming the prioress of some abbey in Connecticut. Right now, Roi thought that was an idea with some merit.

But George Hamilton would sure fit in. Hell. With that tan of his, he could be the patron saint of this place. It was pretty scary.

Even Pico, who didn't fear much of anything, seemed eager to beat a hasty retreat when he dropped them off at the Sands.

"Ay ay," he said to Roi as they finished unloading the bags. "You watch yourself with that *perra*."

Roi was confused. There were no other people around the covered parking area of the hotel. Except for June, the hotel lobby was deserted, too. Roi could see her as she continued to stand patiently by the desk like a nurse obelisk, waiting to enquire about their room reservations.

She looked back at Pico. "Do you mean June?"

"No, bepi. Not the *nurse*." Pico slammed the trunk closed and jerked a thumb toward the lobby of the hotel. "The *mean* one. Inside. La unicornia." He tapped a finger on his temple. "With the coat rack on her head."

"What are you talking about?"

Pico waved a hand. "Never mind. Just remember what I tell you."

"Right. Okay." Roi had no idea what Pico was talking about. She looped the straps of her camera bags over her shoulders and grabbed hold of a suitcase. "I'll keep that in mind."

"I gotta go." Pico pushed his sunglasses up his nose. "You tell your hot *enfermera* that we gonna wrap her key rings 'round the boys tonight." He laughed merrily. "You should thing about unlocking that tall treasure chest of yours."

Roi chose to ignore his suggestion. "You're not coming inside?"

"No, bepi." Pico made a quick sign of the cross before heading for the driver's side door. "I sees you on the flip side."

"Wait." Roi fumbled for her wallet. "Let me give you a tip."

"You wanna tip me?" Pico was already halfway inside the car. "Do it in bills. *Twenties*." He started the car. "Miz Fay can bring you to my show."

He hit the gas and roared out of the parking garage, trailing a plume of dark gray exhaust.

Roi stared after the flame red Delta 88 until it disappeared around a corner.

Okay, that was surreal.

Not that anything else about this trip had been normal . . .

She sighed and wrangled their bags up the steps to the lobby. It looked like the desk clerk had finally shown up. Or, at least, Roi thought she was the desk clerk. She was wearing a blousy, un-tucked denim shirt and had a Scarlet Knights ball cap pulled down over her forehead. She did not look friendly, and she did not look happy to be there. She stood behind her wooden fortress and glowered at June, who appeared to be in the middle of an explanation. Roi drew closer and could see that the unhappy woman was wearing a nametag. "Pauline," it proclaimed in an oddly festive-looking font.

Right now, the *enfermera* didn't seem very cheerful, either.

"I'm sure it's a simple mistake." June pushed a folded piece of paper across the countertop. "Our reservation was for *two* rooms—as is indicated on this confirmation."

The desk clerk didn't bother looking at June's confirmation sheet. She didn't bother apologizing, either.

"It doesn't matter *how* many rooms you think you reserved. This is Women's FEST weekend. Everything in Rehoboth Beach is booked. To the gills."

There was a ding, and they heard the sound of an elevator door opening. Six androgynous-looking women wearing fanny packs and sensible shoes came around the corner and made their boisterous way toward the parking lot.

"I rest my case." Pauline frowned at them. "So, as I was saying. We have *one* room. Two double beds. Full ocean view. Take it or leave it."

June exchanged a nervous glance with Roi.

"Are you certain there are no other hotels in town with vacancies?" she asked the testy clerk.

"I'm positive. Now if you want to try your luck with some of the places further down the beach toward Ocean City, you can probably find something."

"Ocean City? How far away is that?"

Pauline snorted, but didn't reply.

"It's about an hour away," Roi chimed in.

"Unless you hit traffic," Pauline added. "And trust me. You will."

"June. We don't have a rental car. And all the venues are right here in town." Roi faced Pauline. "Could we take a look at the room?"

Pauline sighed and rolled her eyes. She reached into a drawer and pulled out a card key. "This will get you inside. You can leave your bags here while you go up and check it out." She scribbled a number on a slip of paper. "Here's the

Pauline Polito

room number." She pointed over her shoulder. "The elevator is behind us. Take it to the fourth floor, and turn right."

Roi took the card and slip of paper from her. "Thanks, we really appreciate your helpfulness."

Pauline glared at her like she was trying to determine whether or not the comment was sarcastic. In the end, it appeared she didn't really care enough to try and figure it out. She lowered her eyes and resumed working on some papers that littered her workspace.

Roi took hold of June's elbow. "Come on. Let's go check it out."

The elevator door resembled the entrance to a closet, and the elevator car behind the door lived up to its promise. It was dark and very small.

Roi pushed the button for the fourth floor, and the door closed.

There was something weirdly intimate about being close to June in such a tiny space—even more unsettling than the proximity they had shared last night in their roomette. Maybe that was because in here, Roi could actually *see* June's face . . . and all the rest of her, too. She looked pretty stunning in her tailored suit—not at all like she'd been sitting in the thing for more than ten hours.

She smelled great, too. Like ginger and . . . soap.

How the hell was that possible?

Roi also noticed that she looked terrified. Like they were on their way to face a firing squad. She kept fidgeting with the flap of her bag—almost like she wanted to get something out of it, but kept changing her mind.

The elevator was moving at a snail's pace. For some reason, it stopped on every floor, even though no one else was waiting on it. Every time it came to a halt, Roi could sense June's agitation increasing.

She decided to try and distract her. She slapped a hand against one of the dark, faux-wood paneled walls.

"I wonder how all of those women rode down in this thing?"

June looked around the tiny car. "Maybe they took the stairs?"

Roi gave her an ironic look. "I doubt it."

"Why?"

"Let's just say they didn't seem like the stair types."

"Types?"

"Yeah. You know . . ." Roi waved a hand.

June was looking at her with a curious expression.

"You *don't* know. Do you?"

"Apparently not."

The elevator came to a slow stop, and the number four button illuminated. Finally.

They turned right as directed and walked down a swath of faded carpet toward the room. It was located at the very end of the corridor. Roi swiped the card key and they stepped inside.

The room was small and unremarkable, but very clean. And it seemed to be fairly well equipped with all the usual amenities. There were two double beds, separated by the inevitable nightstand, a desk, and two side chairs. The best feature of the room was its view. Roi opened the sliding door that led to a small balcony.

"Wow. This is gorgeous." She stepped outside and leaned on the railing. Only a few people were out walking or jogging along a pristine boardwalk that seemed to extend for half a mile in either direction. The late-afternoon sun was dropping behind the hotels that fronted along the ocean, and they were all casting long shadows across the sand. The tide was coming in. Off in the distance, Roi could see an exuberant Golden Retriever chasing after the retreating waves.

Roi could taste the salt in the air. The breeze off the ocean was perfect—brisk but not too chilly.

She decided that there were worse ways to spend a few days.

June stepped outside to join her.

Far worse . . .

The breeze pushed June's hair around her face in a crazy

confluence of red eddies. Roi had to fight the temptation to reach out and straighten it. June reflexively flipped her head to force her mane of hair back over her shoulder. Roi thought it was about the sexiest thing she'd ever witnessed. She tightened her hold on the balcony railing and did her best to feign indifference.

"So. What say you? Think we can make this work?"

June sighed. "The view is breathtaking."

It sure as hell is . . .

Roi cleared her throat. "Look at the bright side. We have ten times the space we had on the train." She looked back toward the room. "Make that twenty."

June smiled. "I guess you're right. And it is only for three nights."

Three nights? I'll never last three nights. Not if she keeps looking like this . . .

"Right," she said instead. "You stay put. I'll go get our bags."

June gave her a shy smile. "Okay. Thanks for putting up with me."

Roi nodded. She knew she needed to say something, but she suddenly felt incapable of stringing together any combination of sounds that would be intelligible.

June rested a hand on her arm. "Are you okay?"

Roi stared down at June's hand. It felt like a branding iron.

She knew she had to say something. June was scrutinizing her with that full-frontal nurse look of hers

"I'm just . . . *hungry.*" It was lame, but it was the only explanation she could muster.

June smiled. "Well, I think we can take care of that." She withdrew her hand. "Why don't you ask that nice desk clerk for some nearby restaurant recommendations?"

Nice desk clerk?

"Right. I'll do that." Roi took an awkward step backward and slammed into the sliding door.

Jesus. Get a fucking grip.

"Sorry," she said, righting herself. "Back in a flash."

She turned on her heel and hurried out of the room.

Outside in the corridor, she was tempted to stop and bash her head against a dingy, painted wall. She was acting like a horny adolescent. It was ridiculous. She had nothing in common with June Magee.

Correction. With June Magee, R.N.

Whatever.

Roi punched the elevator button.

None of that mattered. They were completely incompatible. And June was straight. *Painfully straight.*

In fact, June Magee was just about the *straightest* woman she'd ever met. The stalwart, media goddess-of-healing could be a fucking poster child for straightness.

She probably had half-a-dozen good-looking, golf-playing, Ivy League surgeons climbing all over each other to plant a flag on her starched-white, yummy goodness.

Roi punched the elevator button again.

Where was the goddamned thing?

Probably picking up another load of . . . revelers.

Good god . . . of all places for Max to send them. *A goddamn lesbian theme park.*

She glared at the elevator door again.

Fuck it.

She decided to take the stairs.

ONCE SHE WAS alone, June gave in to her sensation of panic.

Her eyes swept the interior of the small room and stopped on its two double beds. They weren't more than eighteen inches apart. She began to feel woozy and leaned against the dresser for support.

Why was this presenting such a problem for her? It didn't make sense. It wasn't like having to share a room with another woman was all that difficult. After all, she'd done it for four years in nursing school.

But something about this felt . . . different. And that was because something about Roi was different.

Who was she kidding? It wasn't "something" about Roi. It was *everything* about Roi.

It had to be because she flirted with him . . . her . . . last night at dinner. That mortified her. What on earth had possessed her? She never behaved that way. Well. Not since that one night at the Four Farthings Pub when a bunch of residents coerced her into playing a cutthroat trivia game with curiously high stakes. It took her years to live that one down . . . and most of a week to recover from the hangover.

But that had been back in college. And she'd never allowed herself to lose control like that again. Nor had she been tempted to do so.

Not until now.

There was no denying that she'd felt an immediate attraction to Roi—even though she tried hard to deny it because of their apparent age difference. Letty saw through her in a second. But that was nothing new. June never did have much of a poker face.

But the final mortification came last night when she found out that Roi wasn't a man.

Oh, god. She wanted crawl beneath the table. And as much as she wanted to make her feelings go away, she couldn't. It was an emotional vortex. She felt like a tightrope walker with a bad case of vertigo.

Last night in the roomette had been bad enough, but now this?

She gazed miserably at the double beds. How would she ever manage to comport herself in close quarters like this for two more days?

And three nights.

She just needed more time. Time to make sense of her feelings and regain her equilibrium.

She sank down on one of the two upholstered chairs and noticed the large welcome basket sitting on the desk. It was wrapped in cellophane and tied up with bright, rainbow-patterned ribbon. A card attached to the ribbon read "Welcome to Women's FEST! Enjoy this taste of Rehoboth Beach." June tugged it over and peered inside. The basket appeared to contain all manner of goodies: salt water taffy, chocolates, gourmet popcorn, bottled water, scented soaps, flavored lip balm, a bar and restaurant guide, and a newsletter from someplace called "CAMP Rehoboth." Everything a festival-goer could need to enhance their stay.

Everything but peace of mind and a clear conscience.

She wondered if there were any Milk Duds stashed in the basket . . .

She was still trying to figure that out when someone tapped softly on the door. The sound started her and she nearly dropped the basket. No doubt it was Roi, back from the lobby with their bags. June placed the basket back on the desk and got to her feet.

Time to embrace my fate.

She straightened her skirt and walked to the door.

"SO, WE'RE MEETING Miss Jacobs at a bar?"

They were walking up Baltimore Avenue, away from their hotel.

"According to the note she left us," Roi consulted a slip of paper, "MIXX is actually a restaurant. Your *nice* desk clerk, Pauline, said it's supposed to be across the street from CAMP Rehoboth."

"MIXX?"

"Yeah. I think Pico was actually being ironic when he told us that Fay was MIXX'd up. I gather she transacts a lot of business there."

"She sounds like a colorful character."

"From all accounts, she is. And I think she's some kind of icon here in Rehoboth Beach."

"Oh, look." June pointed at a sign posted in the tiny front

yard of a white frame house. "CAMP Rehoboth. This is where my talk is on Saturday."

"Do you wanna go inside and check it out?"

June thought about it. "No. I think we should go on and connect with Miss Jacobs."

She waited while Roi snapped a few photos of the house.

It looked homey and inviting—almost like a private residence. But then, most of the businesses they passed seemed to exude that same kind of warmth. The majority of them were painted in bright colors drawn straight from a rainbow palette—almost as if the town had a decorating motif.

Yes. The coastal town just seemed . . . *gay.* June smiled at her unintended witticism. Rehoboth Beach was both metaphorically *and* literally gay.

Roi had completed her mini-photo shoot. She looped the camera strap back over her arm and neck and pointed at something on the other side of the street. "MIXX. There it is. And things seem to be hoppin'."

June didn't quite manage to hide her smile.

"What?" Roi gave her a confused look.

"It's nothing."

"Oh, come on." Roi's camera still wasn't settled right. She continued to shift the strap around. "What did I say?"

"It wasn't what you said—it was *how* you said it."

Roi gave her a blank look.

"Your southern accent. It's so sweet when it creeps out."

"Oh, god." Roi rolled her eyes. She gently touched June's elbow and they continued along the street. There were more people milling around down at this end, and it appeared that the majority of them were headed for MIXX. "I don't know if I'd call that sweet. I've tried really hard to lose it."

That surprised June. "Why would you want to lose it?"

"You're kidding me, right?"

"No. I think it's charming."

"Charming?" Roi gave a bitter-sounding laugh. It's about

as charming as that horn Pauline has." She shook her head. "Poor kid."

"Horn?"

"Yeah. Right here." Roi pointed at the hairline above her left eyebrow. "You mean you didn't see it?"

June's stared at her, confused.

"Oh. That's right. You *didn't* see it. She had a hat on when you were talking with her."

They were crossing Baltimore Avenue with a group of boisterous women. June thought she recognized several of them from the lobby of the hotel. They were laughing and bumping into each other as they walked along. She noticed that several of them seemed to be staring at Roi with undisguised interest.

That last part disturbed her. She found behavior like that to be rude and . . . unsettling.

She shifted her attention back to Roi. "Pauline has a growth on her head?"

Roi raised an eyebrow. "You might say that. Now I know why Pico referred to her as *la unicornia*."

"That's not very charitable."

"No," Roi agreed. "But you have to admit that her manner is hardly pleasing."

"She may just be having a bad day."

"Or a bad decade."

One of the portly women bumped into Roi and nearly knocked her back into the street. She immediately proceeded to make a grand ceremony out of apologizing.

"Are you going to MIXX?" she gushed in a rich, alto voice. "Let me buy you a drink to make up for my clumsiness."

A couple of her companions snickered.

"It's okay." Roi held up a hand. "Really."

The persistent woman wasn't ready to give up yet. "Are you here for Women's FEST?"

Roi sighed. "Yes, we are."

Fay Jacobs and Windsor

The woman gave June a good once-over. Again. She bent closer to Roi. "Is *she* family, too?"

Roi didn't reply right away. "No," she finally said. "This is June Magee, R.N., the keynote speaker."

"No shit?" The woman's eyes grew wide. "Hey, girls? This is that famous nurse." She looked at June. "I didn't recognize you without your cape thing."

Cape thing?

June smiled at her. "I only wear it for ceremonial occasions."

Roi shot her a quick glance. June tried hard to keep a straight face.

"I get that." The nosey woman nodded in solidarity. "It's the same way in the National Guard."

Roi cleared her throat. "If you ladies will excuse us, we're late for an appointment." She took June by the arm and steered her toward the restaurant.

"Ceremonial occasions?" she asked, once they had stepped through the street doorway and descended the few steps to the lower-level restaurant.

June shrugged.

Roi shook her head.

"What?" June asked.

"I just never thought you'd joke about your . . . vestments."

"My *vestments?*"

"Well. Yeah."

"Becoming a nurse isn't like taking holy orders," June explained. "I don't risk censure if I appear without my habit."

"Oh, really?" Roi leaned closer. It was very loud inside the bar. And crowded. People were clustered around tables and packed into high-backed booths. Above the din, she could hear music playing. It sounded like Bobby Darin. "Does that mean you won't wear it tomorrow?"

"Of course I'll wear it tomorrow. I'll be working."

"What about right now?"

June smiled. "Right now, I'm *not* working."

Roi seemed about to say something else, but she never got

the chance. A short, dark haired woman wearing black slacks and a loud-patterned blouse rushed over to them. Her ensemble seemed to match the decibel level of the interior.

"Let me guess," she said. "June Magee and Jimmy Olsen?" She laughed merrily and thrust out a hand. "I'm Fay. Welcome to Women's FEST."

Roi and June exchanged glances. June shook hands with the small, bespectacled woman. "It's a pleasure to meet you, Miss Jacobs."

"Oh, sweetheart. Call me Fay. I haven't been called Miss Jacobs since my last pap smear." She paused and looked June up and down. "But in your case, I might make an exception. Do you make house calls?"

June was embarrassed and uncertain about how to reply. Fay just chuckled and turned to face Roi. "And you must be the *Mercury's* legendary photographer." She pumped Roi's hand up and down. "I'm a big fan of your work. That series you did on the fast food worker's strike was stellar."

"You saw that?" Roi sounded surprised.

"Hell, yes. I nearly gave up burgers. Fortunately, god provided Zagat's, so I can still find places to get them if I wait forty-five minutes and pay on the installment plan. Who knew you could do ground sirloin on layaway? It adds a whole new dimension to our trips in the RV."

Roi didn't get a chance to reply because Fay had shifted her focus back to June.

"And you? What's it like to be the only woman on the planet who gets props for wearing white after Labor Day? I tried that once and Bonnie told me I looked like a clearance sale at Bed, Bath & Beyond."

"Well, it's not really intended to be a fashion statement . . ."

"Oh, honey. Name me one cultural icon who set out to become a cultural icon?" She held up a hand before June could reply. "And Cher doesn't count. That woman is packing more wax than her likeness at Madam Tussaud's." She waved an arm toward the booth where she had been seated. "Come on over and sit down. I'll introduce you to the best thing about life in Gayberry, RFD."

They followed her through a maze of revelers to what plainly was *her* table.

"Sit. Sit. Take a load off. I'll order us some refreshments." Fay picked up her martini glass and swirled its contents around. June was captivated by the color of her drink. It was a translucent magenta—not quite blue, and not quite red. It looked like a liquid bruise.

June suspected that too many of them would probably yield the physiological equivalent of the same result.

Fay noticed her studying the drink.

"You need to try one of these," she said. "My doctor told me to drink at least six of them a day."

Six?

"Really?" June tried to mask her horror.

"Sure." Fay drained her glass with a flourish and set it back down on the table. A lone blueberry rolled around inside its bowl like a pinball. "They call it a Faytini. It's loaded with antioxidants, which, supposedly, are great for the memory—which might be true, but I can't recall. Still, I won't look a gift horse in the mouth."

June was nonplussed.

"What's the matter? You've got that same, wild-eyed look I had when my XM Radio got stuck on the Sex Channel."

"She's not much of a drinker," Roi volunteered.

"We can fix that." Fay waved a hand to catch the bartender's eye, and held up three fingers. "Ginger's got the cure for anything that ails you."

June somehow doubted that. When she caught Roi's eye and she smiled at her, she was sure of it.

Fay was watching the two of them. "You two don't get out much, do you?"

"To be truthful," June was trying hard to maintain her composure, "I've never really attended an eclectic event like this one. I'm not really sure what to expect."

"I've always found it best not to expect anything. That way, you're never surprised or disappointed."

Roi chuckled. "That sure would've been useful advice for the ride down here from Philadelphia."

"Why?" Fay looked back and forth between them. "Did something happen during the drive?"

Fay was clearly anxious about their trip. June found her concern to be genuine and charming. She wanted to say something to put her at ease.

"No, no. Nothing went wrong. Pico was perfectly . . . proficient."

"*Pico?*" Fay looked confused. "Didn't Bonnie pick you up?"

June and Roi exchanged glances.

"No," June said slowly. "It was a very . . . accommodating . . . young man named Pico de Gallo."

"Pico de Gallo?" Fay repeated. "I don't know anyone named . . ." She closed her eyes and slapped a hand to her forehead. "Oy. You mean Bonnie sent *Bobbie* to get you?"

"Bobbie?" June looked nervously at Roi, then back at Fay. "No. We didn't meet anyone named Bobbie."

"Let me try to refresh your memory." Fay leaned forward and held her hand several inches above the tabletop. "About six inches tall and built like a swizzle stick? Dresses like Barbie's little sister? Talks like Ricky Ricardo on an estrogen patch? Wears sunglasses the size of a car windshield?" She waited for some signs of recognition. "Am I getting close, here?"

"That sounds like him," Roi offered.

"God." Fay sank back against the wall of their booth. "No wonder you two look like you just escaped from the circus." She laughed and seemed to reconsider her observation. "What am I saying? You just *arrived* at the circus."

"But he told us his name was Pico de Gallo." June insisted. "He said he was an . . . entertainer . . . at one of the local clubs. I think he's South American, although I couldn't quite pinpoint his accent."

"South American?" Fay shook her head. "That's sure a new way to describe Oyster Bay."

"Oyster Bay?" Roi asked. "You mean Long Island?"

Fay nodded. "Although his mother is from Argentina—so props on nailing the accent. Even though he does tend to crank it up."

June was still confused. "He's not a dancer?"

"Oh, no, honey. He's a dancer all right." Fay chuckled. "This week."

"What is he the rest of the time?" Roi seemed to be having less difficulty taking it all in.

"When he's not down here, reinventing himself—a pastime I wholly endorse, by the way—he's a third-year graduate student in medicinal chemistry at Rutgers."

June was stunned. "Pico?"

Fay rolled her eyes. "His real name is Bobbie Brooks."

"Bobbie Brooks?" Roi chuckled.

"Yeah. He's fond of saying his biggest complaint is that his parents—both doctors, by the way—named him after a line of cheap women's clothing." She shook her head. "I think if they'd named him something like Estée Lauder he'd probably be working the runway circuit in Paris, instead of schlepping test tubes in Jersey."

June was still trying to make sense of it all when the server arrived with their cocktails.

"Ah, reinforcements." Fay beamed at the server. "Thanks, doll."

The server mumbled something unintelligible. June glanced up at her and noticed that her lips looked terribly puffy. After she'd deposited the drinks and walked off, Fay tsked.

"Kids these days. Why they all think they need to look like Angelina Jolie is beyond me."

"What do you mean?" June asked.

"The duck lips." Fay used an index finger to draw a quick series of tiny circles around her mouth. "No wonder the lipstick counter at CVS always looks like it's been carpet bombed. I should buy stock in Revlon."

June studied their server as she delivered a tray of drinks to a nearby table.

"I don't think that's collagen," she said to Fay.

"No?" Fay shrugged. "I guess you're right. They use butt fat now, don't they?" She took a sip from her martini glass. "Bonnie said I should give up writing books and become a donor." She slapped her hip. "She says I'm sitting on a gold mine."

Roi choked on her drink.

June was too preoccupied to notice. "There's too much swelling near the vermillion line."

"Near the what?" Fay asked.

"The vermillion line."

Fay squinted. "Is that the one that runs from Chinatown to Glenmont?"

June blinked.

"I think she means the lips," Roi clarified. "On the server."

"It looks like some kind of rash," June added.

"Oh. *That.*" Fay waved a hand. "She's not the only one. It must be making the rounds. She's the fourth one I've seen today."

Raucous laughter burst forth from a table across the restaurant. It wasn't the first time the antics of that group caused heads to turn. The top of their table was loaded with glasses and empty bottles.

"They seem to be having a good time," Roi observed.

"Oh, that crew?" Fay laughed. "They're here for the festival. I think they're sub-letting that space for the weekend."

That piqued June's curiosity. "Really? Who are they?"

"Well, as much as they look like an ad for a twelve-step program, they're authors."

"Authors?"

Fay nodded. "You'll meet a lot of them tomorrow at

your reading. The others will be in some of the sessions on Saturday."

Roi watched the lively group of women work on building a pyramid out of empty martini glasses. It was pretty impressive. "Any names we'd recognize?" she asked Fay.

"Let's see." Fay ticked them off. "Going left to right, the one on the booster seat with the perfect hair is Lynn Ames. The woman wrapped in crime scene tape is Ellen Hart. The one in the blaze orange tie-dye with the seriously great tats is Jessie Chandler. The bossy redhead hugging her single malt is Barrett. The tall one with the hat and the glitter is Bobbie's cousin, Michelle—the festival's official fashionista. Those last two who are passed out on the edge of the booth are Ann McMan and Salem West . . . I think they got shipped here as freight."

June was intrigued. Ellen Hart was the author of the mystery she'd borrowed from Letty. "Is that really Ellen Hart?"

"In the flesh. Do you want to meet her?"

June demurred. It wasn't like her to behave like a fan girl. "Maybe tomorrow."

"That can work, too." Fay pushed a menu across the table. "How about some dinner? The brisket burger here is the best. Then we'll walk over to CAMP and get you all registered. You can pick up your schedules and get your goodies."

"Goodies?" Roi asked.

"It's something new this year," Fay explained. "Some of the local merchants kicked in on a Best-of-Rehoboth gift basket. Pauline and her crew put them all together for us. There's actually some great stuff in it."

"Pauline?" June asked.

"You know her?"

"Well, no. I was just wondering if you meant the young woman who works at our hotel. We had a gift basket in our room when we checked in, so I wondered if there was a connection."

Fay nodded. "That sounds like her work. Her name's Pauline Polito. She's new to the area."

Roi cleared her throat.

Fay noticed. "I see you've met her, too?"

"I'm just surprised that she was involved in helping with the festival." Roi shrugged. "She didn't seem to have much affinity for . . . well . . . for anything, really."

Fay didn't disagree. "I think she's had a rough go of it. It's easy to lose sight of how difficult things still are for a lot of these kids when you live in the Rehoboth bubble. It can be hard to remember that much of the world is still a pretty inhospitable place."

Roi didn't reply.

"Why do I feel like I'm preaching to the choir, here?"

Roi smiled at her. "Is it that obvious?"

"Not as obvious as the horn on Pauline's forehead—but a lot of us wear our scars on the inside."

June was captivated by their exchange. She'd spent the better part of twenty-two hours with Roi in exceedingly close quarters, but somehow Fay had managed to connect with Roi on a more personal level within the space of about twenty minutes. She was beginning to understand why Fay Jacobs was such an esteemed figure in this tiny resort community.

"Don't worry about it, honey." Fay was still talking. "We're all walking wounded. That's where Women's FEST comes in. It gives us all a chance to get together for a few glorious days in this brilliant and beautiful place, perched right on the edge of the world. All so we can be exactly who we are in this grand celebration of the differences we share, and the love that binds us all together."

June was speechless. She stole a glance at Roi, who appeared to be pretty moved, too.

"Pretty good, huh?" Fay reached into her messenger bag and pulled out a glossy flier. "It's off the back cover of our new CAMP Rehoboth brochure. I think it's some of Bonnie's best work." She beamed at them. "Now. How about those burgers?"

THERE WERE ONLY a few people out strolling along the boardwalk when they got back from dinner and their check-in at CAMP Rehoboth. It wasn't quite dark yet, and Roi thought it would be a good opportunity to bag a few background shots for the story of June's visit to the seaside resort.

They left their hotel and walked south on the boardwalk. Roi particularly wanted to get some photos of Dolle's, the legendary salt water taffy shop. It was a landmark in Rehoboth Beach and she knew it would be difficult to find a more iconic backdrop to showcase June's appearance there.

Plus she really liked caramel corn, and Dolle's was reputed to be the best.

She thought it incredible to walk along this pristine swath of oceanfront and recall how it looked during the aftermath of the Ash Wednesday Storm of 1962. She remembered studying those pictures in J-school. A. Aubrey Bodine, the renowned *Baltimore Sun* photojournalist, had taken many of them, and Roi was a big fan of his work. The devastation along this stretch of the Atlantic coast had been epic. The perfect, early-spring storm pounded the area through five consecutive high tides, and left little standing in its wake. Their hotel, The Atlantic Sands, had been among the casualties, too. The boardwalk had been completely destroyed. But, miraculously, the feisty locals had managed to rebuild it before the start of the tourist season that summer. The vitality of this entire area was a stunning testament to the resiliency of the human spirit.

"You seem lost in thought."

June's contralto voice was so soft that Roi barely heard her over the sound of the waves.

"Sorry. I was just thinking about how all of this looked fifty-two years ago."

"Fifty-two years ago?" June was perplexed. "Why?"

"There was a massive Atlantic storm. It completely destroyed all of this." Roi spread her hands apart to encompass everything around them.

"Really? That's incredible."

"It was incredible. And horrible. The storm surge lasted nearly three days."

"How do you know so much about this?"

"One of the newspaper photographers who covered it was someone whose work I've always admired. In my opinion, his photographs rank right up there with the WPA work of Dorothea Lange."

"I'd love to see the images."

Roi smiled at her. "Maybe we can find something in the bookstore tomorrow. If not, I'm sure the local public library will have good documentation. It was the seminal event in the life of this, and nearly every other, Atlantic coast town in the last century."

They walked along in silence. A few other couples passed them and smiled. Roi was relieved that they didn't run into that omnipresent group of festivalgoers again. Twice in one day was already more than enough.

"Don't you find it amazing that a town can have a spirit and a conscience—just like an individual?"

Roi looked at her. June's profile was silhouetted against the blue-black, not-quite-night sky. Brilliant slashes of purple, pink, and orange blazed across the intersection of ocean and sky on the horizon behind her. A last, stray beam from the setting sun managed to snake its way down one of the long city boulevards and illuminate her face like a key light.

Perfect. It was perfect. *She was perfect.*

"Stop," she commanded. "Don't move. Stay *right* where you are."

June froze.

Roi swung her camera up and started shooting. She kept snapping photos until the sun retreated behind one of the behemoth hotels.

God, the woman was born for this. She had perfect features, and the camera loved her. Through the lens, June seemed to melt into the landscape and take her rightful place among the attributes of earth, air, water, and fire—like a grand fifth element.

"Are you finished?" June's question seemed tentative, almost awkward.

Roi lowered her camera and apologized. "Sorry. You have to grab those opportunities when they present themselves. If you don't, they never come around again."

"I guess I know what you mean. The same thing is true in most areas of life."

They resumed walking. Dolle's was just ahead.

"You've had missed opportunities?"

"Of course." June nodded slowly. "Lots of them."

"Why do I find that hard to believe?"

June looked at her. "I don't know. Why do you?"

Roi felt embarrassed by her knee-jerk comment. "I'm sorry. I didn't mean to offend you."

"I'm not at all offended." June gave her a shy-looking smile. "Why do you find it hard to believe that I've had missed opportunities?"

"I don't know. Maybe it's because you seem so . . . comfortable with who you are."

June didn't reply right away.

Roi worried that she'd managed to say the wrong thing again. She opened her mouth to offer another apology.

"I think that what most people perceive as comfort in my demeanor is just an outward expression of my professional persona," June said. "I take my work and the responsibility that goes with it very seriously. That leads me to present with a confidence that I generally lack in my private life."

Roi was unprepared for such candor. She was intrigued that June had opted to crack open a door and allow her a glimpse of what lay beyond the limelight. But she wasn't sure about how far she could push the envelope.

And she really wasn't sure about why she *wanted* to—but she knew she did.

She decided that since June was willing to risk honesty, she could do the same.

"I thought I had the market cornered on insecurity."

June smiled. "I think it's a market with multiple corners."

"Just our luck. Insecurity is a dodecahedron."

June laughed. "I think you're the first person I've ever met who could make geometry funny."

Roi bumped her shoulder. "I think *you're* the first person I've ever met who could notice."

They'd reached Dolle's. It was still open, and its bright, red-orange neon sign vibrated against the sky.

"Here we are." June sighed. "Where do you want me?"

Responses rolled through Roi's mind like the tumblers on a slot machine. She was pretty sure that none of them added up to any kind of winning combination.

Roi looked up and down the boardwalk.

"How about you retrace your steps about fifty feet and walk back toward me?"

"All right." June turned on her heel and headed back toward their hotel. Her path was illuminated by a string of lampposts that ran along the ocean side of the boardwalk.

Roi watched June's form grow smaller as it moved in and out of the white circles of light. The tide was slowly pulling itself back away from the shore. The waves made soft sounds that were more like whispers than anthems.

As ordered, June reached the outer marker of her retreat and began her slow walk back. Roi raised her camera and started shooting. The light was perfect.

Through the lens, June became part of the ageless and unspoiled beachfront. She wasn't so much a creature of this time; she was more a creature of *every* time. June Magee wasn't a misfit—she was a perfect fit. That universal quality of hers—that ability she had to meld without issue into the center of any and every situation—had to be the source of her populist appeal. The nurse was beloved by people of every generation and walk of life for a reason. Photographing her now against this backdrop of a scene that recalled a simpler time brought all of those epiphanies roaring to the surface in a grand explosion of light.

Roi had had quick flashes of these insights before, but never for enough time to distinguish their contours. June with the little boy in the Amtrak lounge. June standing beside the monster locomotives that would pull them both through a sleepless night. June gazing at the ocean through the tangled curtain of her hair. And now, June moving toward her along this fabled boulevard.

Understanding cut through the haze of her subconscious in the same way the orange-red neon of the Dolle's sign cut its way through the advancing night. They were like the tides: moving toward each other, and then retreating. The analogy was so strong that Roi half expected June to reverse her course and drift backward along the wooden platform. But she didn't. She kept advancing. And Roi kept shooting.

When June closed the distance between them, she stopped and gave Roi a shy-looking smile.

"Did you get what you needed?"

Roi wasn't sure about how to reply. "I think so, for now."

"For now?"

"Sure." Roi gestured toward the sky. "The light's about gone."

June nodded. "Were you interested in buying anything here?" She pointed at Dolle's. "It looks like they might be closing."

"Maybe some caramel corn. Unless there's already some in that gift basket?"

June smiled. "You know, I do believe I saw some."

"Any Milk Duds?"

June blushed.

Roi was confused. "Did I say something wrong?"

"No, of course not."

"So I guess you want to take a pass on the candy?"

"I think it's a good idea."

Roi smiled at her. "I agree. It probably would just keep you awake, and after last night, I think we could both use a good night's sleep." She thought briefly about the double beds upstairs in their room.

No . . . there probably wouldn't be much rest for either of them tonight, either.

June just nodded but didn't say anything. They slowly continued on their walk back toward the hotel.

Roi chuckled.

June looked at her. "What is it?"

"I was just trying to imagine this place in the height of the season."

"It is beautiful here."

"True. But I was thinking about how it would look overrun with a couple thousand clones of Bobbie Brooks."

"Chemists?"

Roi thought June's response was literal until she saw the half smile tugging at the corner of her mouth. "Did you just make a joke?"

"What do you think?"

There it was again—that elusive demeanor of hers that walked a tightrope between irony and coquettishness. These random flashes of contradiction blazed across her normally composed features like lightning, and they rarely hit the same place twice.

"I don't know what to think."

"You don't?"

Roi shook her head.

"I guess that makes two of us."

June didn't say anything else, and Roi didn't feel inclined to press her to elaborate when she wasn't even certain what they were talking about—or around.

By the time they got back to The Sands, the tide had reached its lowest ebb. Now the unending cycle would begin all over again.

Roi was about to comment on that when a door banged open ahead of them. Pauline Polito stormed across the outdoor patio area like a thundercloud. She wasn't wearing her ball cap, so the growth on her forehead glowed in the white light like a piece of alabaster.

Unicornia. That's what Pico called her. It wasn't a very charitable description, but as hard as she tried, Roi found it impossible not to stare at the protuberance.

She felt June's elbow press into her side.

"Good evening, Pauline," she said. "Are you off duty for the night?"

Pauline fixed them both with a look that could only be described as a glower. She ignored June's question.

"You got a delivery," she said. "Some kind of booze. I took it up to your room."

"Really? How sweet." June smiled at the bad-tempered desk clerk. "We weren't expecting anything, were we?"

Roi shook her head.

Pauline didn't bother to elaborate. She pushed past them and headed south on the boardwalk with hunched determination. She was wearing boots, and her heels banged out a quickstep cadence that could have heralded an advancing infantry assault.

"That is one twisted sister."

June looked at Roi with an expression that was a combination of surprise and disappointment.

"Not because of her . . . thing." Roi raised a hand and tapped at her own hairline. "Because of her bad attitude. I could care less about her extra appendage."

They watched Pauline's dark form disappear into the distance. When it dissolved into the night, Roi wondered for a moment whether it actually had been there at all.

"*Cornu cutaneum.*"

Roi looked at June. "Excuse me?"

"*Cornu cutaneum,*" June repeated. "That's what her appendage is called."

Roi felt like a schmuck. "I hope you know I wasn't trying to be offensive?"

"Of course I do. Pauline's condition seems like a fantastic aberration, but it's actually a lot more common than you might realize. However, it is odd to find it in someone so young."

"Common?" Roi was incredulous. "The only other time I've seen one of those, it was in a glass jar on display at the Mutter Museum."

"Most people have them removed before they grow that large."

"Can they be removed?"

June nodded. "Although it's best to do so before they're so developed."

"I wonder why she hasn't taken care of hers?"

June shook her head. "It's impossible to say. She could have dozens of reasons."

Roi tried to imagine why anyone would choose to live with such a prominent disfigurement—particularly if it were treatable. It just didn't make sense to her. *Pauline* didn't make sense to her.

"I guess when push comes to shove, it's hard to say whether her surly disposition is because of the horn, or whether the horn is just the outward expression of her innate crankiness."

June actually smiled at Roi's assessment. "Medicine and metaphors rarely go hand in hand."

"Ah, but metaphors are the tools we simpler folk use to understand the relationship between cause and effect."

"Sometimes, there are no relationships. Things just happen the way they happen."

Roi wasn't willing to concede the point. "Without a catalyst?"

"Oh, no. There are always catalysts. But catalysts don't necessarily have value, or proceed from some predetermined purpose. Generally, the meanings things assume are later inter-pretations—applied de facto."

Roi smiled at June. "Aren't we arguing the wrong sides of this issue?"

"What do you mean?"

"Well," Roi leaned against the back of a nearby lounge chair, "it seems likelier that I would be the hardcore realist, and you would be the romantic."

"Medicine is a science. Does that automatically make me a hardcore realist?"

Roi chewed her bottom lip. "I have a hard time imagining that any part of you is hardcore."

"I'm not really sure that's a compliment."

"Believe me. It is."

June's face was wearing that look again . . . that troubled one that telegraphed her lack of composure.

Roi mentally kicked herself. God. Why was it so hard to stay away from the perimeter of this woman's emotional chasm? She all but had billboards posted that blared "beyond this point, there be dragons." But still, Roi kept right on creeping closer and closer to the edge, straining to get a peek at whatever lay just beyond the clearly defined safe zone.

"I'm sorry," she said. She tried to infuse the two words with as much sincerity as she could muster.

"What ever for?" June asked.

Roi waved a hand. "For making you uncomfortable. I honestly don't mean to, but I just seem to keep right on doing it."

June slowly shook her head. "You don't make me uncomfortable."

"I don't?"

"No. I make myself uncomfortable."

"Why?"

June didn't reply.

Roi rolled her eyes. "See? I just did it again."

June gave her a shy-looking smile. "Why don't we just go inside?"

"Right. Because *that'll* sure calm us both down."

"Look at the bright side."

"Which is?"

"Pauline indicated that our delivery was some kind of alcoholic beverage."

"True. But you don't really drink."

"Tonight I might make an exception."

A loud burst of laughter cut through the air. She looked in the direction of the sound and saw the noisy group of women they'd encountered earlier outside the bar. They were weaving their way along the boardwalk, heading for the hotel. It was plain from their uneven progress that they were feeling no pain. And one of them was walking like she'd just ridden a horse across country.

"Oh, god." She took hold of June's elbow. "Let's get inside and hijack that closet-sized elevator before they see us."

"Why?" June looked amused. "Aren't you interested in hearing any of her combat tales?"

"Trust me. The kind of combat she has in mind has nothing to do with her time in the National Guard."

June raised an eyebrow but didn't reply.

They hurried across the pool area and entered the hotel, well ahead of Roi's presumptive suitor.

JUNE WAS HOLDING her tumbler up against the sky, so the amber liquid inside it would be visible in the moonlight.

They were sitting on the small balcony outside their room. It was chilly, but not uncomfortable. Their view of the ocean was perfect. Roi sat across from her on an identical, metal chair. She'd removed her shoes and had her sock-clad feet propped up against the railing.

June took another small sip of the fragrant beverage. It was like vanilla, with hints of jasmine and honeysuckle. It was bitter and sweet, and it warmed her insides like an internal flame. She decided that she liked it. A lot.

"What did you say this was?"

Roi smiled at her. A slightly lopsided smile, with just that one dimple—almost like she was afraid to really commit to it in case she needed to draw it back at any moment. "It's cognac." She picked up the bottle and examined the label. "A very good one, too. Fay has great taste."

"What makes a cognac good?" June didn't really care—she just wanted to hear Roi talk. Her voice was like the drink—soft and slow. Especially when she relaxed and allowed her southern accent to creep out. June just loved those wonderful combinations of lilts and drawls and that style of speaking that made the present tense indistinguishable from the past.

"Aging, mostly," Roi explained. "And, of course, the true cognacs are all from the Cognac region of France. This one is a VSOP—meaning it was in an oak cask for at least four years."

"And I take it that's a good thing?"

"Are you enjoying it?"

"I am." June took another small sip.

"Then it's a good thing."

June smiled at her. "Do you like it?"

Roi took a minute to answer. "Yes, I like it a lot." She sounded distracted.

"Are you all right?"

"I'm fine."

June thought Roi sounded like she was anything but fine, but she was feeling a little fuzzy around the edges and she didn't really trust her judgment. She could tell that the cognac was making her giddy. She wanted to be careful not to let it make her stupid—or reckless.

She cleared her throat and set her tumbler down on a small table.

Roi nodded toward the ocean. "It looks like the tide is turning."

June watched Roi watching the view. Yes. The tides were turning, all right. So fast that it was hard to tell up from down.

The breeze off the water was blowing Roi's dark hair around. She kept shoving it back off her forehead, but it was pointless. As soon as she finished resettling it, the wind shifted it right back to where she didn't want it. June fought an impulse to help her try and straighten it out.

"Are you nervous?"

June stared at Roi with alarm. Had her thoughts been that transparent? She tried to make her tone as neutral as possible. "Am I nervous about what?"

"Tomorrow," Roi clarified. "The signing at the bookstore."

"Oh, that." June tried not to sound as relieved as she felt. "No. I'm pretty used to these events by now."

"Max keeps you on the road a lot, doesn't he?"

"He has ever since the book came out. I gather that these speaking tours help generate revenue for the paper."

Roi laughed. "That's an understatement."

"What do you mean?"

"June. You must know that you've pretty much, single-handedly saved the newspaper from bankruptcy?"

"Oh, I think that's probably an overstatement."

"Trust me, it isn't. Max is an unapologetic skinflint. He knows that you're the most valuable asset the *Mercury* has right now."

June didn't reply right away because Roi looked like she wanted to add something, but she never did.

"If my book and my column have helped the paper and all the fine people who work for it, then I'm very gratified." She gazed out at the ocean. The waves were kicking up more of a ruckus coming in—almost like they were demanding notice that they were advancing and not retreating.

June was feeling bolder, too.

"Besides," she added. "I enjoy these little jaunts to new and interesting places. I sometimes get weary of my life in Chicago."

Roi smiled. "You miss Dairyland?"

"Are you making fun of me?"

"No," Roi said quickly. "Not at all." She picked up the bottle and poured another ounce or two of the fragrant beverage into each of their glasses. June didn't really trust herself

*"I learned a long time ago that I couldn't remake myself.
So instead of trying to hide or fit in, I chose to embrace
my differences. Sometimes I fit; more often I don't.
But I always know who I am."*

to drink more, but she didn't want to refuse Roi's gallant gesture either. "It might surprise to you learn that I actually miss Asheville." She gave a bitter-sounding laugh. "It sure as hell surprises me."

"It's hard sometimes to separate a place from the memories that glom onto it like barnacles on the underside of a ship. One really has nothing to do with the other, yet in our minds, they become inseparable."

"And deadly." Roi nodded. "Ever try to scrape a barnacle off a boat? Those things will slice your hands to ribbons."

"Sometimes, it's better to just buy a new boat."

"You mean make more memories?"

June nodded. "Or different ones."

"It's not always that easy."

"Few things in life worth having are."

Roi looked at her as if she were trying to see through her. "Did you minor in psychology?"

"No. But I have lived longer than you."

"Not that much longer, I'll warrant."

June smiled. "How old are you?"

"Why Nurse Magee." Roi raised an eyebrow. "How very forward. Normally, I make women buy me dinner first."

June could tell she was blushing. She was relieved that the darkness concealed it. "I didn't mean to be so forward."

Roi laughed. "This time, I *was* making fun of you. I'm sorry. I'm thirty-five."

June was surprised. Roi's boyish appearance made her seem so much younger.

"Well?"

June looked at Roi. "Well, what?"

"*Quid pro quo*, Clarice. I tell you things, you tell me things."

"Oh." June smiled. "I'm forty-two."

"A bona fide fossil!" Roi proclaimed. "However do you drag yourself from stem to stern?"

June slowly shook her head. "I never said I was *ancient—*

just that I had lived longer. Which you now must own to be true."

"Right . . . a whole *seven* years. *My god.* What wonders hath been wrought in those seven years? Let's see . . . there was the discovery of fire, followed by moveable type, the steam engine, a cure for polio . . ."

June rested a hand on Roi's forearm. Roi stopped her litany and dropped her gaze to June's hand. Then she met her eyes.

"It ain't the years, it's the mileage," June quoted.

Roi narrowed her eyes. "It seems that we have more in common than our taste in films."

"I know." June withdrew her hand. "It's kind of eerie."

"I think it's great." Roi raised her glass and toasted the ocean. "Up yours, Max. It looks like your little experiment failed miserably."

"What are you talking about?"

Roi faced her. "Oh, come on. You have to know that Max picked me for this assignment because he thought we'd hate each other."

June blinked.

"Seriously? That thought never occurred to you? Pairing the gender-bending, boi photographer and the starched white emblem of Normal Rockwell's America?" Roi shook her head. "I can just see that asshole sitting behind his desk, putting this concoction together like some scheming mad scientist. It's precisely the kind of little experiment he'd whip up, just to get his jollies and find a creative new way to torment you."

"I'm hardly an emblem of Norman Rockwell's America— or of anything else, for that matter."

"Please don't be offended. I'm talking about *Max's* view of reality—not anyone else's. Although . . ." Roi looked her up and down. It was disconcerting . . . and it elicited the same internal response as the cognac. "For my money, you certainly could have held your own on the cover of *The Saturday Evening Post*."

June chose to ignore that observation. It just felt safer. "Why does Max want to torment me?"

Roi drained her glass with a flourish. "My two cents? He resents the hell out of the fact that you and your column have catapulted his newspaper from the trash heap to the winner's circle faster than he can slap a tick."

"Max has ticks?" June picked up her glass and took a small sip. "I could help him with that problem."

Roi laughed. "See? This is precisely what he doesn't get about you."

"Well, to be fair, I think this is precisely what many people don't get about me. And I have to admit that I haven't done much to correct the impression."

"Why is that?"

"Because underneath it all, I really am that misfit from Dairyland. I told you earlier today that being a nurse is not like taking holy orders, but that's not entirely true. For me, it really is. I don't put on the uniform. I *am* the uniform. It's not a job, it's a calling—and the world today no longer has a category for that. We change our careers like we change our hairstyles. You don't like who you are? No problem. You can alter your profile with a few mouse clicks." She looked at Roi. "I learned a long time ago that I couldn't remake myself. So instead of trying to hide or fit in, I chose to embrace my differences. Sometimes I fit; more often I don't. But I always know who I am."

Roi didn't reply, and June worried that she'd said too much. It wasn't like her to be this loquacious. It had to be the alcohol. She cursed herself for being such a lightweight . . . and for her transparency. One of her hallmarks was her ability to retain her composure in almost any situation. So why did she constantly fall short with Roi?

She just needed to stop talking. *That was it.* She talked as a way to fill the emotional vacuum that seemed to open up whenever they were alone together. Talking led to sharing, and sharing too much was what got her into trouble.

Like right now.

She'd revealed too much, and Roi was stuck figuring out a way to respond.

"You know what?" Roi's voice startled June. "I've never heard a more perfect description of how I made peace with my sexuality."

June stared at her, speechless. She felt flustered, and wasn't sure how to reply.

"I hope that didn't offend you," Roi added.

"Of course not. Why would that offend me?"

"Well." Roi shrugged. "I know you were shocked to discover that I'm not a man."

Shocked was probably the least of the emotions she'd felt . . .

"I wouldn't say shocked, exactly." June chose her words carefully. "*Embarrassed* would be more apt." *And mortified would be even more accurate.*

"Why embarrassed?"

June felt her heart rate increase. This conversation was going from bad to worse. She stared down into her glass like she expected to find a safe response floating there.

"Was it because you flirted with me?" Roi asked, softly.

June closed her eyes. *There it was.* Not a safe response, but a truthful one.

And here they were, alone together on a pint-sized balcony that overlooked the edge of her known world.

The waves below them were gaining in intensity. The roar they made was practically indistinguishable from the noise in her head. She needed to look at Roi. She needed to retake control of the conversation. It was easy. She'd done it hundreds of times before. This situation was no different. Admitting her humanity was easy.

It was confessing her vulnerability that was impossible.

"It's okay," Roi said. "You don't have to say anything. It's not the first time I've been mistaken about something like that. I guess I just wanted to believe that you found me attractive."

She laughed. "Now it's my turn to be embarrassed. I guess we're even."

No. June was horrified. They weren't even. Not by a long shot. She wanted to tell Roi that she was wrong. That she *did* find her attractive . . . that she *had* flirted with her . . . with him . . . with *them.* Roi wasn't wrong. Roi was far from wrong . . .

But it was too late. Roi picked up her shoes and climbed to her feet. "How about I go out and scare us up some bottled water that won't give Max an apoplexy? That stuff in the fridge is about six bucks a crack." She looked at her watch. "That'll give you some privacy to shower and get ready for bed. Will thirty minutes be enough time?"

June nodded mutely. It was clear to her that Roi was eager to put some distance between them and this conversation.

"Great," she said. "I'll be back soon."

Roi retreated into the room. A moment later, June heard the door open and close.

She sat staring blankly out at the night. Somewhere, beyond her ability to see, was the line that divided earth from sky. It was the same line that divided day from night, and order from chaos. It wasn't visible now. Nothing was visible now. There were no borders, no boundaries, and no parameters that divided *this* from *that.* There was only a dark, confusing jumble of *everything.* And right now, "everything" was storming her banks like the advancing tide.

But this time, there was a difference. This time, the tide was one June recognized. It was part of the same insistent sea of fear, hope, and longing that had followed her throughout life. The only mystery that remained was whether she'd choose to flee it . . . or, for once, allow herself to kick off her shoes and wade into the surf.

She sank lower into her chair. The only thing she was certain of was that thirty minutes was not enough time to figure it out.

CHAPTER FIVE
Ladies Night

PROUD BOOKSTORE, A direct descendent of the fabled Lambda Rising chain, was one of the last, best independent bookstores. Its inventory was a lively combination of books, magazines, cards, clothing, knick-knacks, and all things LGBT. It was also host to this first leg of June's appearance at Women's FEST.

Six other authors were reading from their books throughout the day. Once they finished, they'd all be available to answer questions and sign autographs. The storeowner, Jacque, had done a commendable job displaying the towers of books written by the participating authors. Fay Jacobs was on hand to moderate the event and perform the introductions.

Roi was impressed by the turnout. The store was filled to the gills with rainbow-clad festivalgoers. She was very relieved not to see her admirer in their midst, although she recognized several other members of that group. More men than women were actually in attendance, and although that surprised her, she didn't take long to figure out why. Most of the men were waving large "What Would June Do?" fans and clutching hardback copies of her book. June Magee appeared to be something of a gay icon in these parts, and her appearance today was generating a lot of excitement.

Roi noticed Pico right away. He was standing near the front of the store, talking in a very animated way with the tall, glittery woman who'd been at MIXX last night. They seemed to be comparing footwear. Roi remembered Fay saying that this was Pico's cousin from New Jersey.

Correction: this was *Bobbie's* cousin from New Jersey.

Pico noticed her and gave a series of exuberant waves before making his way across the store.

"Hola, bepi. I see that you and the nurse survive your first night at the Gay Games." Pico slid his enormous aviator shades down his nose and looked Roi up and down. "And it don't look like you is walkin' like John Wayne, neither—so I'm guessing that you and Miz Annette Funicello each stay on your own sides of the bed last night?"

Roi rolled her eyes. "Hello there, *Bobbie*."

Pico slapped Roi on the arm. "Stop with that Bobbie mess. My cousin tell me that Miz Fay ratted me out to you—but it don't matter. Nobody here knows me as Bobbie. At least, not this week." He pushed his shades back up and scanned the room. "Ay ay . . . you noticing all the duck lips going on around here? Any more and they gonna have to get a wetland license for this joint." He fanned himself with his oversized WWJD placard.

In fact, Roi *had* noticed the thick-lipped trend among the female attendees. But like Fay, she'd just assumed it was some kind of weird cosmetic thing.

"What do you think that's about?" she asked.

"Beats me. But it ain't limited to just the top set of lipses, if you know what I mean." Pico pointed toward his groin area. "That's why I say you ain't walkin' like The Duke."

"I have no idea what you're talking about."

"Oral genital contact, bepi. Sauce for the gooses . . . you know?" He pointed at his crotch. "Down there . . . in the lady basement."

"You mean you think there's some kind of allergic thing going on?"

"All I know is I ain't seein' no fat lipses on any boys. And none of them is walkin' all spread eagle like they's carrying a load in their drawers . . . all except them South Jersey boys on Poodle Beach, and they don't count cause they're packin' socks. Miz Fay says they gotta figure somethings out cause the Lesbanese is checkin' out faster than ants in a Roach Motel."

Roi opened her mouth to reply, but didn't get far because Fay stepped forward to call the proceedings to order. She introduced each of the authors by name, and when she got to June, a loud whoop and holler rolled through the store.

Pico leaned closer to Roi as the cheering went on and on.

"You needs to come to the Lagoon tonight, bepi. Is going to be an all-nurse revue."

"A what?" Roi wasn't sure she'd heard him correctly.

"An all-nurse drag show." Pico pointed his fan at June. "Bring the *enfermera*. I'll save you front row seats."

June at a drag show?

Roi snapped several photos of June standing there, resplendent in her white uniform, as she bowed and smiled at the cheering crowd.

On the other hand . . . why not? It would be great fun—and she'd get some fantastic footage for the story.

"What time?" she asked.

"The show start at nine, but come early for drinks."

Roi nodded and lowered her camera. "We'll be there. Now I have to go to work."

"Ay ay . . . unicornia just come in. *Me tengo que ir.*"

"Pauline is here?" Roi looked toward the street entrance. "Where? I don't see her." She turned back to Pico, but he was gone.

There's just something weird about those two . . .

Roi went to work, moving around the store for the best vantage points. Each of the authors got ten minutes to read, and another ten minutes to answer questions.

Fay had June read last, wisely intuiting that she would be the big-ticket item for this venue. When she finished her prepared remarks, a dozen hands shot into the air. June called on a beefy-looking man with a deep tan and spiky hair that was accented with dramatic blonde highlights.

"I just love your book," he gushed. "And I wanted to ask if it's true that Oprah and Gayle are really lovers?"

June sighed and assured him that she really had no idea.

She called on another, much shorter, man who made a ceremony out of pushing his way to the front of the crowd.

"I read in *OK!* that you still use Breck Shampoo, and have an exclusive product endorsement from Vermont Country Store. Is that true? And if it is, will they ever start selling Breck again in stores?"

Roi chuckled. The look on June's face was priceless. So was the fact that most of the shots she was taking had her framed against a colorful backdrop of Poodle Beach gear.

June good-naturedly answered a handful of similar questions. Finally, one brave soul raised her hand and asked June if she knew anything about . . . rashes.

"What kind of rashes?" June asked.

The woman was clearly finding it difficult to speak. Her lips were terribly puffy and covered with tiny blisters. She pointed a finger at her mouth. "This kind," she muttered.

"Rashes can be caused by all manner of stimuli," June explained. "How long have you had this condition?"

The woman shrugged. "It started yesterday, but today it's a lot worse."

"I'll need a bit more information from you. Would you be willing to remain behind, so we can talk privately?"

The woman nodded.

June gave her a reassuring smile and thanked her before shifting her attention back to the remaining dozen or so hands that were still wildly waving in the air.

When all the questions had finally been answered and the book-signing portion of the event was about to start, June took advantage of a short recess to seek Roi out.

"I know we said we'd get lunch together when this session ended, and I'm sorry it's dragged on for so long."

"No problem," Roi said. "I got some great stuff, and it looks like you sold a ton of books."

"I'll still need to speak with this young woman after the signings," June explained. "And I don't know how long that will take. If you'd like to go on without me, I'm sure I can catch up with you later on."

Roi noticed that two of the women from the group at their hotel were still milling around in the courtyard outside the bookstore. She got an idea.

"No," she told June. "You take all the time you need. I'll just hang around outside. It's a gorgeous day, and I won't have any problem finding something to do until you're free."

"Are you sure?" June asked.

Roi smiled at her. "Positive."

June nodded and walked back to join the other authors.

Roi packed up her camera and made a beeline for the duo outside. They noticed her right away.

"Hey, there," Roi said as she approached. "Did you all enjoy the readings?"

The two women nodded enthusiastically. They each held a copy of June's book.

"Where's your pal?" Roi tried to make the question sound casual.

"Which one?" the shorter of the two women asked.

"The one who talked with me last night outside MIXX? I think she's in the Guard?"

"Oh. You mean Cindy?"

"Cindy. That's right." Roi looked around the sunny, outdoor space. "I don't see her anyplace."

"Oh, well, she's still at the hotel."

"Yeah," the taller woman added. "She's not feeling too well today."

The shorter woman elbowed her friend. "We'll be sure to tell her you asked about her, though."

Roi smiled at her. "Please do." She addressed the taller woman. "You said she wasn't feeling well? What's wrong with her?"

"She's got some kind of monster rash all along the insides of her . . ."

Her friend flashed her a look. "She just had a little too

much partying last night . . . you know how it is when you get a few nights away from the grind."

"Sure," Roi agreed. "Where are you girls from?"

"Columbus," they said in unison.

"Ohio?" Roi asked.

They nodded.

"I'm from Chicago."

"We know," they replied.

"Well," Roi said. "Please tell . . . *Cindy* . . . that I asked about her."

"Oh, we will," said the short one.

Roi raised a hand in salute. "See you girls around."

She could hear them talking in hushed tones as she walked off.

Something strange is totally going on around here. She raised a hand to her mouth and touched her lips. *I sure hope it isn't in the water.*

She walked along the outdoor mall that ran between the rows of tiny storefront shops until she found an unoccupied bench, and sat down to wait for June.

THE TIME WAS well past the lunch hour, and Roi was starving. After nearly three hours in the bookstore, she was ready for some space and some quiet.

They walked along Rehoboth Avenue, looking for a good place to eat. A sidewalk sandwich board outside a café called The Cilantro Cantina caught Roi's eye, and she stopped to look it over. A woman was outside near the entrance fussing with some potted plants and noticed them standing there.

"This is the best food in Rehoboth Beach," she declared. "Authentic. Every dish is made by hand."

"Do you serve alcohol?" Roi asked.

The woman stared at her like she'd just been asked to prove she had opposable thumbs.

"Of course," she said. She waved an arm toward the door. "Come in. Come in."

Roi and June exchanged glances and meekly followed the bossy woman inside.

"Sit down. There." The proprietor pointed at a small table. "What do you want to drink?"

Roi ordered herself a mango margarita, and a Ketel One Cosmopolitan for June. June raised an eyebrow, but didn't protest. Roi also asked if the woman could suggest a good appetizer.

"All of my appetizers are good," she said.

"Will you choose one for us, then?"

She nodded. "I'll send you some Queso Fundito en Cazuela."

"Thanks. We'll order some food after we have our drinks."

The woman walked off.

"Cosmo?" June asked.

Roi shrugged and smiled at her. "You earned it."

"I'm not used to drinking so early in the day." June laughed. "Who am I kidding? I'm not used to drinking *any* time of day."

"Or night?" Roi quipped.

"Or night," June agreed.

"I wouldn't worry too much about it. You seem to be holding your own."

"That's a matter of opinion."

"Right. That's my opinion, and I'm sticking to it."

June smiled.

They had a nice table inside the restaurant, but situated next to an open-air seating area outside along the sidewalk.

June was perusing the menu. "This food looks extraordinary."

"She said it was all authentic," Roi reminded her. "How hungry are you? It's so late in the day that we could actually make this our evening meal—unless you have other plans."

June gave her a curious look over the top of her menu. "I don't have other plans. At least, none that don't include you."

Roi smiled. "That's good to know. Especially since I more or less committed us both to attend an event later tonight."

"You did?" June put down her menu. "What kind of event."

"Um." Roi took a big sip of her margarita. "Pico was at your reading."

"Yes, I saw him there. It was very sweet of him to attend."

"Right. Well, he invited us to a . . . show. Later. At his club."

"A show?"

Roi nodded.

"What kind of show?"

"He said it was a revue."

"A revue?"

Roi nodded again.

June narrowed her eyes. "What kind of revue?"

"A . . . um. . . *nurse* revue." Roi cleared her throat. "An all-nurse revue."

"What on earth is an all-nurse revue?"

"It's, um . . . well . . . it's a drag show. Kind of. An all-nurse drag show."

June's eyes grew wide.

"It's in your honor," Roi clarified. "So I felt I had to accept."

June dropped back against her seat. "I have no idea what that even means." She fixed Roi with a distressed gaze. "What is an all-nurse drag show?"

"You've never been to a drag show?"

June shook her head.

"But you understand the basic concept, right?"

"Of course."

"Well. Think of it as your typical drag show, only with a common, thematic element."

"Nurses?"

"Right."

"They're all going to be dressed like nurses?" June clarified.

"Well. Not nurses, per se. It's likelier that they'll all be dressed like . . . um . . . you."

"Me?" June looked incredulous.

Roi nodded. "But with slightly more pronounced . . . foundation . . . garments. And with less . . . *utilitarian* . . . footwear."

June rolled her eyes and took a big swallow of her drink.

"And . . ." Roi continued.

"And?" June glared at her.

"Eye makeup," Roi added. "Lots and *lots* of eye makeup."

June drained her glass. "Can I get another one of these?"

Roi stared at her open mouthed.

The server arrived to deliver their appetizer and to take their orders.

"Yeah. We're gonna need another round." Roi pointed at June's empty glass, then handed her the menus. "And would you just ask the proprietor to select something for us?"

"Are either of you vegetarians?" the server asked. "Any food allergies?"

Roi shook her head.

"Just shellfish," June said.

"Okay." The server smiled at them. "We'll have something special for you right up." She picked up June's empty martini glass and headed off toward the bar.

June still looked shocked.

"Look," Roi leaned over the table and lowered her voice. "It's intended as a compliment. A . . . tribute, really."

"A tribute?"

Roi shrugged. "Sure. Think about how hard it is to find white stockings in a beach town. And queen size, at that."

June responded with a small smile.

Roi went in for the kill. "It would mean the world to Pico to have you attend."

June sighed. "Against all sense and better judgment, I suppose you're right."

Roi smiled and relaxed.

"But I have a condition." June raised an index finger.

"What?"

"No photos."

No photos? Was she kidding? The photo op was the only reason Roi agreed to go.

"June . . ."

"No. I mean it. No photos. I'll go, but I won't participate in something that lampoons a noble profession."

"June. The fact that it *is* a noble profession is what makes it a suitable theme for a drag show."

Roi could tell by June's expression that she wasn't buying it.

"Think about it. How many drag shows have you seen that feature serial killers or crack whores?"

June sat back and folded her arms. "I thought we'd already established that I haven't seen any drag shows?"

"I rest my case. That fact itself gives the experience of going journalistic merit. And we need to document all aspects of your visit. It's about what will benefit the paper, June. That's why we're here. And this event will allow you to reach an entire new audience. It's not a lampoon, it's an affirmation."

June sighed and shook her head.

"Well?" Roi asked. "What do you think?"

"I think you could sell ice to an Eskimo."

Roi grinned at her. "Great. Eat up . . . It's gonna be a long night."

When their entrees arrived, they were plainly the house specialties. June's Chiles Rellenos Adelita looked large enough to feed a family of lumberjacks. By comparison, Roi's over-stuffed Taquitos Dorados de la Merced made June's entrée look puny.

They decided to share.

After several bites, Roi asked June about her consult with the thick-lipped woman at the bookstore.

"So, can you tell me anything about it, or would that be a HIPPA violation?"

Predictably, June seemed reluctant to go into too much detail. "It appeared to be some kind of contact dermatitis. Almost like an allergic reaction to something. It makes me wonder about any commonalities, since she suggested that so many of the festival attendees appear to be similarly afflicted."

"That's true. But remember the waitress at MIXX had the same issue, and I think she's a local."

"You mean she isn't staying in any of the hotels?"

Roi nodded.

"The rash seems so localized that it probably isn't being caused by anything like soap or shampoo."

"And so far, neither of us has it."

"That's true," June agreed. "But we don't know how long it might take for the effects to present. Everyone is different. And I always travel with my own cosmetic products."

"Well. I don't. So, *great* . . . There's something to look forward to."

"I wouldn't worry too much. Not everyone appears to have it."

"Pico said something to me about other issues cropping up."

"Other issues?"

"Yeah. I mean other . . . areas. Apparently, some women are being affected . . . *downstairs*."

June scrunched her brows together. "Downstairs?"

Roi nodded.

"You mean in the groin area?"

"Yeah. Pico called it the lady basement."

June rolled her eyes.

"While you were in the store talking with your patient, I was outside getting some information about Cindy."

"Cindy? Who is Cindy?"

"You know." Roi waved a hand. "My suitor. From MIXX?"

"Her name is Cindy?" June didn't seem too pleased about this development.

"Yeah. Well. When we saw them last night, I noticed she was walking kind of funny, and Pico's comment got me thinking. So I asked her pals where she was, and why she wasn't at the reading."

"Why?" June asked in a tentative voice. "Are you wanting to connect with her?"

"*No*." Roi glared at her. "Earth to nurse? Jeez. I was trying to get *information*. And one of her pals volunteered that Cindy was down for the count with some kind of rash—in her lower forty-eight."

June sighed. "Could we please refrain from the euphemisms?"

"Okay," Roi agreed. "She has an inflamed hoo ha."

June chewed the inside of her cheek. "You're doing this just to annoy me, aren't you?"

Roi smiled at her. "Is it working?"

"Like a charm."

"Well, euphemisms aside, she apparently isn't the only one with this problem. What do you think?"

"What do I think about what?"

Roi sat back and gestured toward the street. "Come on, June. Connect the dots. Big lesbo festival? An outbreak of rashes on the lips and . . . *lips*? Only women from out of town are affected?"

June held up an index finger. "The waitress at MIXX is not from out of town."

"Well," Roi countered. "Not that we know of. And maybe she hooked-up with somebody who is in town just for the weekend?"

"Possibly," June agreed. "But in any case, what's your point?"

"My point is that this outbreak or allergy seems to be pretty specific and pretty targeted."

"We don't know that. It could just be coincidental."

"Coincidental?"

June nodded. "For one thing, there aren't enough common denominators to be meaningful. All the women are in town for different lengths of time. They aren't staying at the same hotels. They aren't eating the same foods. They aren't all interacting with each other in . . . intimate . . . situations." She looked at Roi. "Are they?"

"How the hell would I know?"

"You seem to have your finger on the pulse of this culture. I mean, based on your eloquent defense of the social relevance of drag shows."

Roi sighed. "Touché. I guess I deserved that one."

"I'm glad we agree on something."

Roi decided to try another approach. "Okay. You examined that woman in the bookstore. What can you deduce about her rash?"

"Like I said earlier. It appeared to be some form of contact dermatitis. It was almost poison ivy like in appearance— except that it presented in a much more accelerated fashion. She also indicated that the rash was better today than yesterday, so it seems to be cycling more quickly."

"And what do you think caused it?"

"I honestly have no idea. Some kind of toxin."

"You said you thought it was some form of contact dermatitis. That means she got it on her lips though direct contact with whatever the culprit is?"

June nodded. "Correct. The rash would appear on whatever body part has direct contact with the toxic substance."

"But nobody has it on their hands?"

"Not that we're aware of. But then, we've hardly made any kind of scientific study, either."

Roi sat back and twirled her fork around and around.

Sauce for the goose. That's what Pico said. She repeated the phrase aloud.

"Excuse me?" June asked.

"Sauce for the goose." Roi bent closer to June over their small table. "*Oral sex.* Wouldn't that be one way to transmit the toxin?"

June blushed.

"Well?" Roi asked.

"*Yes,*" June hissed. "Of course it could be spread that way. But we still don't know where it originated or how so many different women with nothing in common except their

*June's hand shot across the table and grabbed her wrist.
"Wait a minute," she commanded. "Don't open it."*

attendance at the festival came into initial contact with the agent."

"Don't we?"

"I certainly don't. Do you have a theory?"

"Nope." Roi sighed and speared a big jalapeño pepper from June's Chiles Rellenos. She didn't usually care for the hot ones, but today they tasted just right. Maybe that's because she was washing them down with the best margarita she'd ever had.

The only down side was that her mouth was on fire. She tried wiping it with her napkin, but that only made the burning worse.

"You really need to quit eating so many of those," June said.

"You think?" Roi touched her lips to try and cool them off. "Do you have any ChapStick?"

"Sorry." June shook her head. "Just lipstick. But you're welcome to some of that."

"You're an autumn, and I'm really more of a summer." Roi quipped. "So I think I'll pass." Something else occurred to her. She slapped the pockets of her jacket.

"What is it?"

"I grabbed that lip balm from the gift basket . . . I know it's here someplace." She finally found it buried beneath a wad of receipts at the bottom of a side pocket. "Voila." She pulled it out and waved it aloft. "Relief is at hand."

Roi slipped her nail beneath the plastic seal.

June's hand shot across the table and grabbed her wrist. "Wait a minute," she commanded. "Don't open it."

"Why?" Roi looked at June, then at the lip balm, then back at June. June's hand was soft and warm. She had a nice grip.

"The gift baskets," June said. "It's the gift baskets. That's what they all have in common."

"Oh, holy shit." Roi dropped the tube of lip balm to the table. "You're right."

June released her wrist and picked up the small tube.

"You think somebody spiked the lip balm?"

"It's possible." June examined the tube. She held it up to her nose and sniffed it.

"Do you smell anything?" Roi asked.

"Just piña colada—and poblano."

"Poblano? Who would put that in a lip balm?"

"It's not *in* the lip balm." June pushed her plate away. "It's what's left of my lunch. We need to get this out of here so we can really examine it. And we need to compare it to one from the store where it was made."

"How do we do that?"

"Easy." June showed Roi the tiny printing across the barrel of the tube. "It's on Rehoboth Avenue, near the bookstore."

"I'll be damned."

"It says they also sell handmade soaps and lotions."

"Hot damn. I think we're on to something."

"Don't get too excited. It's a long shot, at best."

"At least we now know that MIXX had no involvement."

"What do you meant?"

"They didn't have any role in putting the gift baskets together. Besides," Roi raised a didactic finger, "in my view, any place that sells forty-two types of vodka is practically a shrine."

June rolled her eyes. "I suppose that makes some kind of sense." She was still examining the lip balm. "The reality is that however this happened, we won't get far until we locate a lab that can analyze the compounds."

Roi pulled out her cellphone. "I can take care of that."

June gave her a quizzical look.

"I believe this is a case for Bobbie Brooks, boy chemist and Ph.D. candidate."

"You can't be serious."

"I'm completely serious."

"What makes you think he'd have access to a mass spectrometer?"

"June. This is Delaware. There are chemical plants about every twelve feet."

"So?"

"So . . . one thing our boy Pico has is connections." Roi paused. "Remember Alphonse?"

June blushed.

"I'm confident that we can get him to help us out. Especially if we sweeten the deal."

"What do you mean by sweeten the deal? I'm not sure I like the sound of that."

Roi was already punching in Pico's number. "I'll tell Pico that you'd just *love* to participate in his all-nurse revue tonight."

June's eyes were like saucers. "You most certainly will *not*."

"Hey? You want to pay the piper, you got to dance to the music."

"I think you have that backwards."

"I know." Roi smiled at her. "Don't worry about it, June. Just remember the advice Queen Victoria gave her daughter on her wedding night."

"I'm certain I'll regret asking, but what advice was that?"

Roi grinned. "Close your eyes and think of England."

June started to protest, but Roi held up a hand.

"Yo? Pico? Hey. It's Roi Rodgers. Yeah. Listen man, we need a favor . . ."

AS IT TURNED out, Bruce Burnside, Pico's current inamorata, worked as a lab analyst at Johnson & Johnson in Wilmington. His office was located about ninety minutes away, straight up Route 1. Pico graciously offered to drive them up there tomorrow to drop the item off, but Roi explained that they really needed to go today, while the lab was open. So Pico offered to let them borrow his car. Roi had a momentary qualm about driving the fire-engine-red land yacht, and she worried about re-traumatizing June by reprising their wild ride in the demon machine. But she was wise enough not to look a gift horse in the mouth. She accepted his offer with gratitude.

It didn't take them long to find the lotion shop, and they also were able to grab a couple of unused tubes of the lip balm from left over gift baskets at CAMP Rehoboth.

June felt it was important to clue Fay in on their suspicions. Fay agreed that there were far too many cases of the mysterious rash cropping up for it to be coincidental. Many of the afternoon events had been so poorly attended that organizers were starting to panic. Several dozen couples had already checked out of their hotels and departed early. Fay worried that news of the epidemic would hit social media and spread like wild fire, seriously impugning the stellar reputation of the festival.

"The last thing we need," she said, "is for people to equate Women's FEST with one of those floating Petri dishes they call cruise ships."

Fay also gave them a heads-up about where the gift baskets had been assembled. CAMP volunteers had collected all the donated items from area merchants and delivered the bounty to the Blue Lagoon. Employees of the Lagoon then worked after hours to organize the merchandise, and fill and wrap the baskets in bright cellophane.

It was that simple. The part that wasn't simple was finding out who had the expertise to taint the lip balm if, in fact, it had been tainted—and coming up with a motive to explain why they did it.

June and Roi met Pico at the hotel and he gave them directions to Bruce's lab, and a quick tutorial about some of his car's quirks.

"Okay. The top don't go down no more, so don't try it." He looked at June. "And you don't wanna end up like Miz Jayne Mansfield, neither, so is a good thing."

"Check," Roi noted. "No convertible."

"An the cigarette lighter don't work, neither. So if you wanna fire one up you gotta use the Zippo in the console."

Roi assured him that they wouldn't be smoking.

"It burns oil, so you gonna have to top it off when you gets to Wilmington. I have a six-pack in the trunk. Do you knows how to do this?"

Roi nodded.

"An the speedometer is busted, so is best just to go with traffic. You'll knows if you gets over eighty cause the steering wheel starts shaking like Oprah in hot pants."

"Right," Roi agreed. "No steering wheel shake."

"Don't try no sudden stops." Pico wagged a manicured finger at them. "The brakes don't always work so good."

Roi sighed. "Pico, if we don't head out soon, we won't get there before the lab closes."

"Okay, okay!" Pico handed Roi a key ring that was hopelessly weighted down with bangles and streamers. A round plastic frame containing a miniature portrait of Hello Kitty dangled from a long chain of rainbow-colored beads. "Here you go. Tell Smoochie I sees him later—an he better not be lates."

Smoochie?

"You mean Bruce?" Roi asked.

"Sí. He's coming down for the weekend." Pico slapped Roi on the arm. "Yo, bepi? With luck, maybe I gets to walk like John Wayne, too—only without the rash, you know." He fanned himself. "My Smoochie can go all night, if you knows what I mean."

Roi shot June a nervous glance, but she had already climbed inside the big car. She appeared to be preoccupied with looking around for the seat belt.

Pico bent down and peered at her through the window. "Ain't no seat belts, nurse. You gets scared, you gonna have to hold on to your boi. But she look like she has a lotta good places to grab."

"And we're off." Roi pushed Pico out of the way and climbed inside the car. "Thanks again for this—and for connecting us with . . . Smoochie. We really owe you."

"Yeah, well . . . You pays me back tonight." He leaned down and looked at June. "Nine o'clock, nurse. Remembers to bring the cape."

June gave Pico a polite smile, but didn't say anything. Although Roi was pretty sure she heard a soft sound that was like a whimper.

Roi started the big car and it shuddered to life. Pico waved at them as they drove out of the parking garage and headed up Baltimore Avenue toward the Coastal Highway that would take them to Wilmington.

Once they were clear of the hotel, June let out a deep breath.

"I cannot believe I let you talk me into this."

"What do you mean?" Roi looked at her. The bench seat was roughly the size of a living room sofa. June looked half a mile away. "I thought you wanted to get these samples up to the lab today so we could get to the bottom of whatever's going on here?"

"Not *that* part." June waved a hand. "I mean tonight. The . . . nurse revue."

Roi had trouble stifling a laugh.

June squinted at her. "Don't think I don't know how much you're enjoying this."

"Well. Can you blame me?"

"Let's see." June sat thinking for a moment. "Yes. I do believe I can."

Roi laughed. "I can hardly wait to see what your idea of paybacks is."

"Oh, you won't have to wait."

June crossed her long legs and Roi suddenly got a vivid reminder of all the ways June could make good on her promise.

She gripped the two-toned steering wheel a bit tighter and cleared her throat.

"Maybe it won't be that bad."

June raised an eyebrow. "Really? I think that's the same thing they said about Krakatoa."

June pulled a tiny box of orange Tic Tacs out of her bag and offered them to Roi.

Roi shook out a few of the candies and passed the container back to June. "Look at the bright side. We needed a reason to get into the Blue Lagoon to look for clues about the gift baskets. Now we have a perfect excuse to be there."

"I suppose you're right."

"Of course I'm right."

"Roi?" June asked sweetly.

"Yes?"

"Don't push it."

Roi chuckled. "So, how long will this spectrometry thing take?"

"Not long. We're fortunate that Pico's friend actually works in the lab and knows how to operate it."

"What would the going rate for a test like this be on the open market?"

"A lot more than either of us could afford—ever."

"Really? I wonder what old Max would say if a charge for mass spectrometry showed up on our expense report?"

"He'd probably think it had something to do with hair removal."

"Brilliant! *Waxing.* After all, we are in a beach town."

"Roi?"

"Yes, June?"

"We're not expensing this."

Roi sighed. "How in the hell are we gonna pay for it, then?"

"I've already taken care of it."

"You?" Roi looked at her in surprise. "How did you manage that?"

June smoothed her skirt. "Believe it or not, I get hundreds of offers for product endorsements."

"You mean like Vermont Country Store?"

"Not exactly. That one is apocryphal."

"You mean you're not a Breck girl?"

"Not since junior high."

Roi shook her head. "Damn. Another fantasy bites the dust."

June smiled. "So, I've had several requests to do some print ads for Aveeno white peach and ginger body wash products."

White peach and ginger? Wait a minute . . . that was the scent that clung to June like a second skin. Roi remembered seeing the bottle in their shower this morning. She felt like a pervert because she picked it up and stood there in the hot spray, guiltily sniffing it for more than a full minute.

"Hold on." Roi looked at her. "Don't you use that?"

June nodded. "I always have. I don't know how they found out, but they've been dogging me for months to do the endorsement. I never consented until now."

Roi was confused. "Why do it now?"

"Because Aveeno is owned by Johnson & Johnson."

Oh my god. "You're fucking brilliant."

She shrugged. "It wasn't hard. I just called my agent, and she made the deal."

Roi was still shaking her head. "I can't believe you worked this out."

"I felt I had to. I know that Pico's friend, Bruce, would have tried to help us out on the side, but I didn't feel right about risking his job security if anyone found out about this unauthorized use of the equipment. Laboratories take that kind of thing very seriously."

"You're a good egg, Nurse Magee."

"You would've done the same thing."

Roi waved a hand. "Oh, sure. If either of the Mr. Johnsons needed any free wedding photography or portraits of the family dog, I'd have stepped right up to offer my services."

"Stop it."

Roi was still amazed by June's revelation. "It's incredible."

June was silent.

A thought occurred to Roi.

"So, um . . ." She tried to make her voice sound casual. "In these ads . . . Will you be *using* the body wash?"

June threw a Tic Tac at her. "How about you keep your mind on the traffic?"

"Oh, come on. I'm a *professional*. I'm just curious about how they'll do the photo shoots."

"We haven't gotten that far in the negotiations yet."

"Well, let me know if you need any help."

June raised an eyebrow. "I doubt I will. I've been showering by myself for years."

"That wasn't the part I meant."

Of course, Roi was lying and she suspected that June knew it. "I'll be sure to keep your offer in mind," she said.

They rode along in silence for a few minutes. Roi was amazed at the change in tone their relationship had taken. It was almost as though their forced intimacy had shifted their comfort level with each other into hyper-drive. Odd, since they still tended to tiptoe around each other whenever the conversation turned to anything remotely personal.

Roi blamed herself for that. She had given in to an idiotic impulse last night when she had suggested that June had flirted with her on the train. June's horrified reaction made it clear how off the mark her suggestion had been. She'd wanted to throw herself off the balcony, just so she wouldn't have to keep looking at that terrified expression on June's face.

One thing was for certain: she'd never make that mistake again. She was confident that her attraction to June was fleeting. Temporary. Borne of the fact that the two of them had been unceremoniously plucked out of their daily lives and tossed together into the middle of this frolicsome, gay-topia. She knew that she would never look twice at someone like June Magee under normal circumstances.

Well. That wasn't entirely true.

She tried to steal a covert look at June as she stared out the window at the passing, low-country landscape.

The woman was just hands-down, smoking *hot*. In any day or time. Roi would have to be brain dead or blind not to look at her twice.

Plus she was nice. And smart. She was clever, too, in her low flying, beneath-the-radar way. She never saw her humor coming, but it was always there—just below the surface.

And she smelled like white peaches and ginger . . .

The steering wheel started shaking beneath her hands. She glanced down at it in surprise.

"Jeez." She took her foot off the gas. "Pico wasn't kidding about this thing."

"I wondered why we were speeding up," June remarked. "Are you worried that we won't get to the lab before five?"

"Oh, no. We'll get there in plenty of time. I was just preoccupied and not paying attention."

"I can understand that. This view is kind of unvarying and hypnotic."

Roi agreed. "It reminds me of South Carolina."

"Really?" June sounded intrigued.

"Yeah. Ever been to Myrtle Beach?"

"No."

"Well, there's only one way to get there, and it's on about a hundred and fifty miles of road through country that looks exactly like this . . . only Delaware grows chickens instead of cotton."

"It sounds charming."

"Trust me. It ain't."

"I thought you said there were parts of your life in the south that you missed?"

"There are. But driving for hours along backcountry roads past sharecropper shacks and cement statues of purple Jesus aren't among them."

"Purple Jesus?"

Roi nodded.

"I thought that was a bathtub punch served at fraternity parties?"

Roi looked at her with surprise. "Apparently Dairyland wasn't as backward as you suggested."

"I never attended fraternity parties in Dairyland."

"No? Then where did you attend them?"

"You're making an awfully broad assumption, aren't you?"

"Hey. You brought it up."

"My anecdotal mention of a widely-known cultural phenomenon in no way suggests that I have personal experience related to the activity."

Roi thought about that. "So, that means you went in nursing school?"

"Precisely."

Roi laughed. "Some day, somebody is going to make a fortune writing about *June Magee: The Lost Episodes.*"

"I certainly hope not."

Roi was tempted to suggest that tonight's all-nurse revue would likely warrant a chapter all by itself, but she wisely kept silent.

CHAPTER SIX
I'm Coming Out

IT WAS NEARLY eight o'clock when they piloted Pico's Delta 88 back into the parking garage at The Atlantic Sands. June was exhausted. Two sleepless nights, no dinner, and a lot more alcohol than she was accustomed to imbibing were combining to make her feel more than slightly fuzzy. More than once, Roi had offered to stop along the way back so they could get some coffee and a bite to eat, but June refused.

"I've got a show to do," June had said, "and I don't want to be late."

They barely had enough time to get up to their room to shower and change before heading over to the Blue Lagoon. And June needed extra time to prepare tonight, since she was expected to appear in full nurse regalia—including her *cape thing.*

They agreed that while June was in the bathroom getting ready, Roi would call Fay and fill her in on the results of their trip to the lab.

June had been stunned by the results.

Bruce Burnside's mass spectrometry test showed that the lip balm had been tainted with a foreign substance.

According to the test results, it was an unusual compound. Clearly synthesized, but very similar to the chemical makeup of urushiol. It had been applied topically to the lip balm, so it only showed up on the outer edges of the solid.

Bruce told them that he even had a couple of the other chemists take a look at it, just to confirm the findings. But only the tubes from the gift baskets had been tainted. The foreign substance caused the same allergic response as urushiol. It likely presented almost immediately and subsided more quickly.

It was all so incredible. Someone had tainted the tubes of lip balm with a synthetic allergen similar to the one found in poison ivy. And whoever had done it was skilled enough to ensure that the effects would be immediate, but temporary.

Since festivalgoers had been targeted, the message was clear. But what would make someone want to target gay women? And why would someone want to ruin such a popular festival?

Maybe Roi was right. Tonight, they'd have access to the Blue Lagoon, where the gift baskets had been put together. It was pretty clear the lip balm had been unaltered when it had been delivered from the shop that made it. So the mischief had to have occurred at some point before the baskets had been delivered to the various hotels in town. That meant that whoever was involved in assembling or delivering the baskets was probably involved in tainting the lip balm.

Of course, it was possible that more than one person was involved. According to Bruce, someone with a lot of chemical expertise had compounded the substance employed. That took a special kind of skill.

June wiped the steam off the mirror. This was getting her no place. She only had twenty-five minutes to get ready for her . . . debut . . . at the club. They'd just have to figure it out once they got there.

She stared at her reflection and tried to persuade herself that this was going to be no different from any other public appearance—just a tad more . . . *animated*.

She wondered if she'd have to dance.

What difference would it make? She was positive that none of the lessons she'd taken at Fred Astaire would have relevance for tonight. And even if they had, who on earth would lead?

It was best not to think too much about that part.

And Roi would be there.

With her camera . . .

June closed her eyes. This was going to be a nightmare of epic proportions.

There was a soft tap at the door.

"June?" Roi asked. "I hate to rush you, but I'd like to grab a quick shower, too."

Of course. How selfish of me to monopolize the bathroom. June was embarrassed. "I'll be right out." She could dress and finish her makeup in the room.

She wrapped herself in a skimpy towel—then thought better of it and added a second one.

She walked into the room. Roi was standing by the balcony doors. She was fiddling with one of her cameras. That made June's stomach lurch, but she did her best to appear confident—which wasn't at all easy to do when she was standing there, barely covered up and dripping all over the carpet.

Roi looked up and saw June. Her mouth fell open and the camera slipped out of her hands. She managed to catch it by the strap before it hit the floor.

"I didn't mean to startle you," June apologized.

"Oh," Roi stammered. "I'm not . . . startled. You just look . . . it's . . . I'm . . . I need to hurry up and get ready, too."

"I'm sorry I took so long. I had to wash my hair."

"Right. Your hair. Of course you did. I mean . . . it's really . . . wet." Roi set the camera down on a table. "Do you need the dryer from the bathroom?"

"No. I carry one with me. I'm fine."

"You are. *Fine.* I mean . . . yes . . . that's good. Okay." Roi slapped her hands together. "Let me get in there. A long cold shower is just what I need."

June stood aside so Roi could brush past her. She thought Roi was walking a little unevenly. *The lack of sleep must be affecting her, too.*

"A cold shower?" she asked. "I think there's plenty of hot water left."

"Great," Roi muttered. "I think I need both."

Roi closed the bathroom door and June sagged down on one of the beds.

What on earth is the matter with me? I have got to stop making her so uncomfortable.

She sighed. *Only two more nights of this torture. Then I'll be alone on the train back to Chicago and I can find my equilibrium again.*

Roi had already told June that she'd purchased an airplane ticket for the return trip. She did it before they had left Chicago, she explained. After all, it didn't seem to her that they'd need any footage of the ride back once the festival assignment was over.

June was okay with that plan. Spending too much time with Roi was making her careless. Unguarded. Uncertain. She didn't need those complications. She'd done a stellar job up to now organizing her life to avoid them.

And right now, she had a more immediate concern: to be made-up, dressed, and ready by the time Roi emerged from the bathroom.

She stood up and did what she did best. She went to work.

THE BLUE LAGOON was a gay nightclub known for its great food, stiff drinks, and rollicking live entertainment. Its drag shows were reputed to be among the best on the Atlantic seaboard. On Friday and Saturday nights, patrons would begin lining up outside hours before the shows started. Everyone knew it would be SRO at the Lagoon any night that "Auquanetta Champüe and the Poodle Beach Girls" took the stage.

Roi and June approached the entrance and saw Pico waiting for them at the street. He wasn't in costume yet, but he'd clearly made a good start on his makeup. Roi thought he looked like a cross between Joan Crawford and Cher—mesmerizing and terrifying all at the same time.

"Ay ay, hurry up, hurry up," he gushed. "We gotta gets you insides before this crowd goes loco." He looked June over.

She was wearing a lightweight version of her traditional

cape, so most of her uniform was concealed. Pico pulled one side of the cape open so he could examine her ensemble. "Mmmm, mmmm, nurse!" He bobbled his head from side to side. "You is lookin' hotter than a pot of necks." He dropped the cape and wagged a finger at Roi. "And you, with that whole k.d. lang thing goin' on . . ." He snapped his fingers. "Girl, it's workin'." He grabbed them both by the elbows. "Come on, let's go. We needs to run through the routine at least once."

"Routine?" June asked.

"Don't worry, nurse. The boys do all of the work during the lifts."

"Lifts?" June shot Roi a panicked look.

Roi cleared her throat. "Um, Pico?"

"Later, bepi. It looks like the crowd has seen the nurse."

He was right. It started out as a titter. Then it spread through the dozens of people in line like wildfire. There were a few whoops and whistles, and then the entire assembly erupted into a noisy round of cheering.

Chants of "June, June, June!" and "What Would June Do?" and "Take my temperature!" rang out over the clapping and wolf whistles.

June smiled and waved at the crowd. Dozens of tiny cell phone flashes fired like strobe lights. Roi was pretty sure that June's image would be plastered all over social media before they even got inside the door of the club.

"I'm seriously going to kill you for this," June hissed behind her smile.

"Me?" Pico looked alarmed. "What did I do, nurse?"

"Not you. *Her*." June tilted her heads at Roi.

"You can't kill me. It would violate your Florence Nightingale pledge." Roi swung her camera up and backed off to get a few shots of June against the backdrop of the warehouse-style club exterior and the cheering crowd.

"Yo, hurry up, bepi. We ain't got times for this. Günter is waiting to meet the nurse."

"Günter?" June asked. "Who is Günter?"

"Is Aquanetta." Pico hurried her along. "Her real names is Günter Schmidt."

Roi finished taking her last couple of shots. A very buff-looking bouncer met them at the entrance and opened the door with a flourish.

"I just love your shoes," he whispered to June as they hurried past him.

The club interior was cavernous but unremarkable. Roi thought it looked just like every drag club she'd ever visited. Without people, it felt about as homey as an airplane hangar tricked out with tables and lots of gaudy neon signs.

I wonder if joints like this come in kits, like adult sets of Tinker Toys?

That would explain why they all looked alike, no matter what city you were in.

She wrinkled up her nose. *And why they all smelled alike, too.* One thing Roi hated was the odor of cheap, stale beer.

She noticed that a massive bar area occupied one entire sidewall. An impressive stage took up most of the rear. It was rigged out with theatrical lighting and a runway that extended out into the seating area. Clearly, drag shows were the bread and butter of this establishment, and the Blue Lagoon went all out.

There was a long hallway to the right of the stage, behind the kitchen area. It appeared to lead to the restrooms and club office.

That's where their snooping around for clues would likely take place.

The music inside was already deafening, and that was without patrons. The extended play, dance version of "Disco Inferno" was blasting its way through about its twentieth minute. She couldn't imagine how loud it was going to get in just a few minutes.

Roi saw Pico's multicolored "key rings" strung all over

the place. They were like eclectic Mardi Gras beads—only more . . . utilitarian. She wondered if June noticed them.

She saw June and Pico walking toward the big stage and it appeared that Pico was showing her the lay of the land.

Roi looked around until she found a good table: one that would give her the best vantage point for photos.

It was going to be a long night.

"I didn't expect to see you here." Roi spun around, startled by the voice.

Pauline Polito. She didn't look particularly happy, but Roi was learning that this wasn't an uncommon state for Pauline. Roi smiled at her, just the same.

"I could say that makes two of us."

"I work here," she explained.

"You do?"

Pauline nodded. "In the back. I do the books." She continued to stare at her.

Roi noticed that she was wearing her ball cap.

"Why are you two here?"

"Pico invited us. He asked June if she'd do a cameo in the show tonight."

Pauline rolled her eyes. "That sounds like him. I'm surprised she'd go for it. She seems too uptight to appear in a drag show."

"You think June is uptight?"

"Don't you?"

"Actually, no. She's really one of the most open-minded people I've ever met."

Roi was really just doing her part to defend June, but once the words were out of her mouth, she realized how true they were.

Pauline was giving her a strange look. "You're pretty gone on her, aren't you?"

"Excuse me?"

"You heard me. You and half the women who are in town this weekend."

As annoyed as Roi was by her suggestion, she was also curious about Pauline's observation.

"Half? Why only half?"

Pauline gave a bitter-sounding laugh. "Because the other half is fantasizing about *you*."

"Me?" Roi was flustered. "What are you talking about?"

"I really don't think you need me to spell it out. You two have pretty much owned this place since you set foot in town. If you don't believe me," she waved a hand toward the stage, "ask *Bobbie*."

"It sounds like you know Bobbie pretty well."

Pauline snorted. "Everybody in Rehoboth knows Bobbie."

"So you're not really friends?"

"Not really." She shrugged. "We went to school together. But that was a while back."

"College?"

"What's with the twenty questions?" Pauline looked at her watch. "I'm on the clock. You want to make small talk? You can look me up later at the Sands. I've got the graveyard shift . . . again."

She walked off without saying another word. Roi watched her stride down the long hallway that led toward the restrooms.

What a total bitch, Roi thought. *I don't care if she has had a rough go of it.*

The room started filling up with more than just obnoxious dance music. They had finally opened the street doors, and the club was starting to hum. People were hurrying toward the back to claim seats at the best tables. Roi was glad she'd already scoped one out.

"I need a drink."

Roi turned around and blinked at June.

"Make that *two* drinks," June added, in a weary tone.

Roi smiled at her and pulled out a chair so she could sit down. June carefully folded her cape and draped it over the extra chair that held Roi's camera bag.

"How did it go?"

"Oh, fine. Miss Champüe walked me through the number."
June slowly shook her head. "If I live through this, it'll be a
miracle."

"You'll survive."

"What makes you so sure?"

"Because you've got that rock-solid, heartland, can-do
spirit."

"My rock-solid, heartland, can-do spirit might be useful if
I were preparing to pasteurize cheese. I fear that appearing in
a drag show exceeds the reach of my Dairyland upbringing."

Roi laughed.

"Oh, please." June held up a palm. "Do not even pretend
this is funny."

"Okay. How about I get you that drink?"

June sighed. "You don't have to bother. Pico said he would
take care of it for us."

"Really?"

June nodded. "He's sending us some food, too. I asked for
something light, but god knows what we'll end up with."

Roi opened her mouth to venture a guess.

A server showed up bearing a tray loaded down with plates
and glasses. "Okay. Who got the iced tea?"

June raised her hand.

Roi was surprised. "I thought you said you needed a drink?"

June took the tall glass from the server. "I do, but I think
it's best if I keep my wits about me tonight."

The server chuckled and faced Roi. "So I guess that means
you get the double Crown Manhattan?"

"Um. Yeah." Roi looked at June in surprise. "How did you
know I liked these?"

"It's what you ordered on the train."

"So it is."

"Okay." The server was offloading an array of appetizers.
"Here's some deep fried, goat cheese stuffed ravioli with
marinara sauce. Some of our signature panko crusted chicken
and crudités with bleu cheese dip. And last but not least—a

plate of crab cake sliders and a side of fries." He stood back and tucked his tray beneath his arm. "You folks gonna need anything else right now?"

Roi was too stupefied to speak.

"Yes." June stepped into the void. "Does this establishment have a portable defibrillator?"

The server blinked.

"She's kidding," Roi explained. "We're fine. Thanks so much."

The server nodded and walked off.

"I *wasn't* kidding."

Roi looked at June. "I know. But right now, I'm so hungry I could eat all of this by myself."

June looked over the array of comestibles. "I wouldn't advise it."

"So." Roi took a sip of her drink. It was a good one. Strong. "When's show time?"

"Not until ten-thirty." June was fixing herself a plate with raw vegetables and a piece of the chicken. "They pushed back the start time for the second show."

"You're in the *second* show?"

"Apparently. The only bright side is that it'll give us some time to look around."

"I'm way ahead of you on that one. I just had what passes for a lively conversation with our friend Pauline."

June's eyes grew wide. "Pauline is here?"

"Yeah. And she expressed a similar surprise to see the two of us."

"It's hard to fault her for that."

"True. Turns out she works here."

"Really?" June looked around the club. Even if Pauline had been milling around, it would have been impossible to pick her out. There were just too many people crammed into the place now.

"She does the bookkeeping," Roi explained. "So she's likely in the office."

"Office? Where is the office?"

Roi pointed toward the neon restrooms sign. "I think it's back there someplace."

"Interesting."

"I was thinking the same thing." Roi tried one of the fried raviolis. They were delicious. The goat cheese was blended with something else she couldn't identify. Whatever the combination was, it was working just fine. "You need to try some of these. They're fabulous."

June looked dubious, but she speared one of the morsels and took a small bite.

"You're right. The filling is wonderful."

"There's something else in them besides goat cheese."

June nodded. "Probably mascarpone."

"Mascarpone? I thought that was a kind of sweet, cream cheese. More of a dessert thing."

"Not always," June explained. "It blends very well."

Roi tried another one. The filling was a perfect medley of sharp and sweet. The taste it created was sensational. And it was packed in pasta and *fried*. How much better could life get?

"Wow. I never would've put these two things together."

"That's the wonderful thing about the science of cooking. It's part method, part formula, and part luck."

Roi laughed. "That sounds more like a description of *life* than science."

"I guess that's true." June shrugged. "Sometimes, unlikely combinations have a way of working out in life, too."

"You can say that again. Think about Sonny and Cher."

June smiled. "Abbott and Costello."

"Simon and Garfunkel."

"Mickey Rooney and . . . anyone." June smiled. "Or in his case, *everyone*."

"Road Runner and Wile E. Coyote."

"Bonnie and Clyde."

"Lucy and Ricky."

June took a moment to think. "Can I use Woody Allen for my next three answers?"

Roi folded her arms. "Nope."

"Ogre." June thought some more, and then brightened up. "Boris and Natasha."

"Good one." Roi leaned forward. "Gertrude and Alice."

"Rosencrantz and Guildenstern."

"Wait a minute. They weren't a couple."

"Prove it." June took a sip of her iced tea.

Roi tried to think back to what she knew about the ill-fated pair. Not a lot. In fact, they were really only famous for being dead. "Okay. I'll let that one ride."

"Why are you the one in charge of the rules?"

"I just am." Roi tapped her chin. "Let's see. Ah." She held up an index finger. "June Magee and the Poodle Beach Girls."

June rolled her eyes.

"Well?" Roi asked. "No snappy rejoinder? Does that mean you yield, and I win?"

"I wasn't aware this was a contest."

"Of course it is."

"Okay, wise guy." June leaned over the table. Roi had a hard time concentrating on anything but the sudden close-up of all that tantalizing white real estate, and everything it was having a hard time concealing. "You and me."

"You and . . ." Roi couldn't even repeat it.

June sat back and picked up her iced tea again. "What? No snappy rejoinder? Does that mean you yield and I win?"

Roi was still having a hard time finding her tongue. And it didn't matter anyway, because even if she'd been able to get that part of her anatomy working, her entire vocabulary had just roared out of town on a rocket.

Yeah. They had lift off, all right. Right here, in the middle of a drag bar at one of the gayest beach towns in America.

Roi made a couple of nervous, little nods. "You win all right."

"Good." June gave Roi a blinding smile and drained her glass. "I like to win."

"I'm figuring that out."

"So what do I get?"

"*Get?* Get for what?"

"Winning. What's my prize?"

"There's a prize?"

"Silly girl. There's always a prize." June looked around the club. "Where's that server? I need more tea." She managed to catch someone's eye and held up her glass.

"I'll have to think of something," Roi muttered.

"Good. I can hardly wait to see what you come up with."

"That makes two of us."

What the hell was happening here? Roi felt like they were playing one of those 3-D Scrabble games, where the words changed at every turn. June was behaving like some kind of changeling. Or was she? Roi had already made that mistake before—and it wasn't a scenario she cared to revisit.

She smacked a palm against the side of her head to try and shake its contents back into a configuration that made sense—or at least one she recognized.

"Are you all right?" June asked.

"To tell the truth, I'm not really sure."

"What's wrong?" June was all business now.

The server showed up with June's tea. He also had a second double Manhattan in tow.

"I took a chance and thought you'd be due for another one," he said, "But it looks like you aren't quite ready. Do you want me to take this back?"

"No," Roi said quickly. She made an eager grab for the drink. "I think this is just what the doctor ordered."

The server smiled and departed.

June was still looking at Roi with an intense expression.

"I'm okay," she said. "Let's just drink to a successful evening—on *all* levels."

"Are you sure?"

Roi nodded.

"All right."

They clinked glasses and sipped at their drinks. Well . . . Roi sipped at *hers*. June was taking a sequence of pretty hefty swallows.

"You must have been dehydrated," she observed, when June finally set her glass down.

"It's not that. I get thirsty when I'm agitated. Always have. Of course," June turned on her chair and looked around the club, "my cure for agitation does have a down side."

Roi chuckled. "Are you looking for the restrooms?"

"How'd you guess?"

"Call it a hunch."

"Where did you say that restroom sign was?"

"Back there—down that hallway to right of the stage."

"Right." June pushed her chair back and got to her feet.

Roi was always surprised at how tall June was. Watching her stand up was like viewing one of those time-lapse videos on the Science Channel—the kind that showed a beanstalk going from sprout to full-grown in six seconds.

"Will you excuse me?" she asked.

"Sure." Roi smiled at her. "I'll be right here."

June lightly ran her hand across Roi's back as she walked behind her. It was probably completely innocent. The kind of thing anyone would do in a place that was so damn crowded. But something about it felt . . . intimate. Almost naughty.

Naughty? *What the fuck was the matter with her.*

There was nothing naughty about June Magee, R.N.

She swiveled around on her chair to watch June's progress across the club.

Damn. The place was so crammed with bodies it looked more like the Chicago stockyards than a bar. The only reason she could even pick June out was because of her blinding white form. It moved around and through of the crush of people like a lighthouse beacon. People kept stopping her to shake her hand or gush about something.

Auquanetta Champüe and her Poodle Beach Girls were gonna have one helluva show tonight.

Roi felt like she'd already been treated to one helluva show. She was still reeling from how June looked when she had emerged from the bathroom wrapped only in a couple of those miniscule hotel towels. Good god. The woman was like an artist's model. Roi had no trouble at all imagining her draped across a patterned settee or dancing around a vase of nasturtiums. She was a glorious creature with her long, strong body and all those generous curves in all the right places. For the first time, Roi understood on a visceral level why professional photographers like Herb Ritts chose to spend their careers showcasing the sheer beauty of the human form.

Roi could only fantasize about what it might be like to take this unadorned June—the woman inside all the celebrity trappings—and reveal her . . . as she truly was.

But, no . . . that wouldn't be right. The depth of June's beauty emerged when *she* chose to reveal it, in those unscripted moments that couldn't be manufactured. It couldn't be teased out of her with the right props or lighting. That would be a disingenuous exercise and, although the results would likely be breathtaking, the experience would be one that did credit to neither of them.

This entire trip had been a conundrum for Roi. Since the moment she first met June in Max's office, her emotions had been swinging like a pendulum between extremes of fascination and disbelief. Right now, it felt a whole lot like fascination was winning out. And the most disturbing thing about this trend was the fact that fascination was rapidly morphing into attraction.

I just gotta get through tonight and tomorrow. Then we're outta here, and I'm back on a plane to Chicago, and a life that makes sense.

Roi continued to scan the crowd, but she couldn't spot June's form any longer. There were just too many people standing around in that part of the club.

She finished her first drink and pulled the second one over to take its place. The sound system was blasting another Village People song. She thought about that band's penchant for dressing up as cultural stereotypes. She looked down at her own ensemble and thought about how retro her London Drape suit was. She and June made quite a pair: a couple of square pegs in a sea of round holes. It probably was no accident that one of them was ending up on the stage tonight.

Maybe I should put on a feathered headdress and join the show, too?

Nah.

If I did, they'd probably charge me twenty-four dollars for this Manhattan.

WHEN JUNE EMERGED from the restroom, she experienced a momentary wave of light-headedness. It wasn't like the floor was tilting, but it was disconcerting enough to force her to stand with a shoulder pressed against the wall for a few moments so she could get her bearings.

I probably need to quit being so particular, and eat some of the food Pico sent. My blood sugar is way off.

She looked up and saw the door to the office straight ahead ... and it was standing wide open. From her vantage point, she didn't see anyone inside the small space.

She took a quick look down the corridor that led back to the club. No one was coming. *This was her moment.* She nonchalantly sauntered past the open door and stole a peek inside. It was empty.

She took another quick look down the corridor. It was still void of people. She knew Roi would be annoyed at her for branching out on her own, but this was a golden opportunity that might not present itself again. And, after all, this was why they were here tonight—her drag debut, notwithstanding.

She took a deep breath to try and clear her fuzzy head and crept inside to have a quick look around. If someone caught her, she could always claim that she made a wrong turn trying to find the bathroom.

The small business office was fairly typical with an old metal desk loaded with papers and a desktop computer that had some kind of spreadsheet open on its monitor. The chair was pushed back and swiveled away from the desk. The room also contained a couple of battered file cabinets and some old lockers. Half a pot of coffee steamed on a hotplate that sat atop a small, dorm-sized refrigerator.

She recognized Pauline's bright red ball cap and a messenger bag hanging on a peg next to a partially open door. It looked like some kind of storage closet.

June snuck over to take a peek. The tiny space overflowed with supplies with barely enough room for anyone to squeeze inside. It contained a tool box, various industrial-sized jugs of cleaning products, and a vacuum cleaner with a thick, orange power cord that had to be at least a hundred feet long. Buckets and mops were stashed in the only available corners. Two narrow sections of steel utility shelving were bolted to the outside wall. She wedged herself in to take a closer look. The shelves were loaded down with packs of printer paper in an array of bright colors, business forms, bar rags, Rubbermaid bins full of empty condiment bottles, and a plethora of cast-off calculators.

On the top shelves, she spotted several tied-off grocery store bags, some ribbon, a roll of rainbow-colored cellophane, and a stack of empty baskets. There were also some small, cardboard boxes with "CAMP stuff" written on them in black magic marker.

Bingo. This was the spot all right.

She reached up to pull down one of the boxes and heard voices. She took an anxious look back at the office. The sounds were getting closer. She recognized Pauline's nasally diphthongs. The other voice was unfamiliar to her.

June panicked. She had no way to get out of the office now—or concoct a reasonable defense for being caught skulking around in the club's storage closet.

She hurriedly pulled the door closed, plunging the tiny space into total darkness.

Pauline and whomever she was talking with entered the office. June heard the outer door close.

"I don't give a flying fuck how you figure it out," Pauline hissed. "You told me this wouldn't be serious and now it's turned into a class-A clusterfuck."

"Hey," a male voice replied. "I'm not the one who was balls-to-the-wall bent on making a goddamn statement. All I did was make a fucking phone call. So don't go tryin' to pin this shit on me, 'cause it won't stick."

"Look, asshole. I'm not trying to pin *anything* on *anybody*. I just want to clean this mess up before it gets any worse."

The man snorted. "Ain't it a little late for you to develop a conscience?"

"Fuck you."

"Not the best way to get me to bail your ass out, Paulie."

"You know what? You can just go to hell. I don't need your help."

"Yeah? Well, I'll be happy to see your ugly-ass, back end— just as soon as you pay the rest of what you owe me."

June could hear Pauline let out a long, slow breath.

"You're a real creep, Alphonse."

"You're breakin' my heart, Paulie. Now, gimme the goddamn money. I wanna get back to Chester before midnight."

June could see shadows moving in the strip of light beneath the door. They seemed to be getting closer. Her heart started to pound. There were rustling noises against the wall beside the door.

Ohmygod. Ohmygod. Pauline is getting her bag. She's right outside the door.

June held her breath and squeezed her eyes shut. Now she did feel like the floor was tilting beneath her feet. She knew this was it. Pauline would open the door and they would find her spying on them. And what would they do? Whoever this

Alphonse was, he didn't sound like a very understanding character.

The rustling sounds stopped and the shadows retreated.

"Here's your money. Now get the fuck out of here."

"Fine. Next time you need help with one of your little experiments, you can call one of your Gamma Rho sisters—if you can find any of 'em who will still talk to you."

"Go to hell, Alphonse. You were a loser then, and you're a loser now."

"Hey? At least *this* loser got a sheepskin. All you got is *bounced*."

"I got bounced because *you* set my ass up. I didn't have anything to do with stealing that lab equipment and you *know* it."

"Nice try, pumpkin. Life must be hard with a rap sheet and a shit load of debt."

Pauline didn't reply.

"I almost forgot to mention that little French tickler on your forehead," Alphonse said. "But, hey? Looks like you found a great place to land. Tell me . . . What's it like to satisfy two queens at once?"

June jerked at the sound of slap, followed by scuffling noises and a loud thump.

"Try that again and I won't be so *nice*," Alphonse growled.

"Just get the fuck out of here," Pauline gasped. Her voice sounded muffled—like she was holding something against her mouth. "You got what you came for."

"Do us both a favor, Paulie. Lose my number."

A moment later, June heard the door to the office open and slam shut.

She held her breath. *Did Pauline leave, too?*

She heard snuffling sounds. No. Pauline was still there. *And she was crying.*

June bit her lip. It took every amount of restraint she possessed to remain hidden.

The phone in the office rang. Pauline sniffed a few times and cleared her throat before she answered it.

"What?" There was a pause. "Right *now?*" Another pause. "Fine. Fine. Keep your damn hot pants on. I'll be right up there."

June heard her slam the receiver down. Then the door to the office opened and closed again.

She counted to ten—twice. The office was still deathly quiet.

This was her chance to escape.

She fumbled in the dark to find the doorknob. It spun freely in her hand. The knob was broken, and the door was locked . . . from the *outside.*

ROI KEPT STARING at her watch like she was expecting it to give her different information.

It didn't.

June had now been gone for more than twenty minutes. Something was wrong. *She knew it.* It wasn't like June to just disappear this way. And she had been acting . . . strange, too. Uninhibited. Familiar, even. Some of that made sense. After all, they had practically been on top of each other for the last three days.

She had to suppress a smile at the mental image *that* phrase conjured up. Nope. There wasn't a thing in the world wrong with the idea of being on top of June . . .

Roi tapped a finger in agitation against the side of her glass. Most of the ice had melted in June's iced tea.

What the hell was taking her so long?

She looked toward the hallway for about the hundredth time and caught a glimpse of Pauline Polito pushing her way through the crowd. It looked like she was heading for the pass station.

Roi checked her watch again.

"I thought I recognized you."

Roi looked up at the man who was standing next to their table. It was Smoochie.

"Hi," Roi said. "It looks like you made it in time for the show."

Bruce rolled his eyes. "You have no idea. If I'm even five minutes late, Bobbie has a meltdown that makes Mt. St. Helen's look like a training bra."

Roi laughed.

"Where's your squeeze?"

Roi didn't bother to try to correct him. It was too complicated. "She had to powder her nose."

"So she's in the show tonight?"

Roi nodded. "Under duress."

Bruce smiled. "No wonder this joint is so crowded." He gestured toward one of their unoccupied seats. "Do you mind if I join you—or is this seat taken?"

"Oh, god. No." Roi pushed the chair out. "I apologize for my rudeness. I didn't realize you were looking for a spot. Of course you can join us."

Bruce sat down. "What are you drinking?"

"It's a Crown Manhattan. A pretty good one, too."

"Too rich for my blood." He gestured toward June's glass. "That looks pretty deadly, too."

"No," Roi corrected. "June's just drinking tea."

"*Tea?*" Bruce raised an eyebrow. "The nurse is drinking the Lagoon's tea?"

"Yeah. Why?"

Bruce chuckled. "Did you try it?"

"No. Why?"

Bruce picked up June's glass and passed it to Roi. "Here. Take a whiff."

Roi nervously took the glass and held it to her nose. The fumes about made her eyes water. "*Holy shit.* What the hell is in this?"

"Seriously? I think a little of everything."

Wait a minute . . . this is *Long Island* Iced Tea?"

"No," Bruce corrected. "It's Rehoboth Beach Iced Tea."

"Is there a difference?"

"Oh, yeah. Long Island Iced Tea kicks your ass and drops you in the gutter. Rehoboth Beach Iced Tea kicks your ass and makes you stay up all night singing Gloria Gaynor tunes."

"Oh, god." Now Roi was seriously worried about June . . . What if she were sick? *Or worse?*

"Hey. Would you do me a huge favor?" she asked.

"Sure."

Roi got to her feet. "I'm gonna go check on June. Will you watch our stuff?" She gestured toward her camera and June's bag.

"Absolutely."

On impulse, Roi snatched up June's cape. If June was . . . not herself, she might want it.

"I'll be back in a flash."

Bruce smiled. "Good luck."

Roi nodded and began to fight her way across the club toward the restrooms.

She saw Fay Jacobs and a couple of the festival authors holding forth at a large table. Fay caught her eye and gave her an energetic thumbs-up sign. Clearly, the news about June appearing in tonight's show had managed to travel faster than the urushiol-induced rash they were here to track down.

Roi reached the women's restroom and was almost afraid to go inside. Once she did, she was even more alarmed to discover that June was nowhere to be found. She did, however, find several other women whose open looks of admiration suggested that they'd be more than willing to help her forget any problems she might have. Roi politely begged off and remembered all the reasons why she'd decided to quit clubbing a few years back.

Out in the hallway again, she felt her nervousness increase. The door to the club office was closed. She knew that Pauline was probably still up front taking care of her errand, but she had no idea who else might be working back here. That fact made it impossible to go inside and look around. She leaned against the two-toned wall next to the office door and tried to figure out her next move.

She heard something. Faint, but unmistakable. Tapping. Rhythmic tapping. Three short. Three long. Three short. Then the same sequence again.

Morse code?

Roi turned and stared at the wall. The sequence repeated.

It *was* Morse code. The SOS. *What the hell?*

She looked up and down the hallway before gingerly taking hold of the doorknob. It was unlocked. She slowly opened it and looked inside. The office was empty. Then she heard the rhythmic tapping again. It seemed to be coming from behind another door at the back of the small room.

Oh, Jesus . . . that has to be her. Who the hell else would even know Morse code?

Besides me.

Roi closed the door and hurried toward the source of the tapping.

"June?" she whispered.

"Roi?" an anxious voice replied. "Oh, thank *god*."

Roi opened the door and June spilled out against her. She was blinking furiously and ducking her head to dodge the light. Roi grasped her by the forearms and held her upright.

"What the hell are you *doing* in here?" she whispered.

"I saw the door open when I was on my way back from the restroom," June explained. Her voice sounded husky. "I snuck in to take a look around. Then Pauline came back, and I had to hide."

June was still swaying. Roi tightened her grip on her arms. "Why were you still in here? Pauline's been up front for about the last ten minutes."

"I know. The door locks from the outside and the knob in there is broken."

June was blinking less, but her eyes still looked vague and

unfocused. Roi wasn't sure if that was because of the light or because of her two Rehoboth Beach Iced Teas.

"We need to get out of here before she comes back."

June nodded. Then she narrowed her eyes. "Why do you have my cape?"

Roi glanced down to where it was draped over her arm. "I thought you might be sick, so I brought it with me."

"You came to find me?" she asked in a small voice.

"Of course. I was worried."

June leaned into her. "That's so sweet . . ."

Roi shook her gently by her forearms. "June? Come on . . . We need to get out of here."

"Wait." June tugged Roi back toward the closet. "I have to show you something."

"We don't have time for that. Come on. We need to go."

"No." June continued to pull Roi into the storage area. Even in her semi-inebriated state, she was surprisingly strong, and Roi was having a hard time making headway in their tug of war. She decided that the better part of valor was just to give in and let June have her way.

"Okay. What is it? *And hurry up.* We don't have a lot of time."

June raised her arm and pointed at the top of some metal shelves. "Up there. Look."

"What? What am I looking at?" Roi cast more nervous glances toward the door to the office than at anything inside the closet.

June took hold of her face and turned it toward the shelves. The sensation of having both of June's hands on her face was not an unpleasant one. It occurred to Roi that being in here might possibly be worth the risk of discovery.

"Look," June said again. "*Up there*. Baskets. Cellophane. Boxes of CAMP stuff. This is what we were looking for."

Roi saw it all now. "Holy shit. You're right."

June nodded energetically. "And that's not all . . ."

The door to the outer office cracked open. Roi clamped a

hand over June's mouth and hurriedly pulled the door closed behind them.

"Hey, Pauline? Hold up," a voice called out. "I need another one of those register tapes."

"Hang on," Pauline replied. "I've got an extra one here in my pocket."

Roi and June were plastered up against each other in the small, dark space.

"Great," June whispered. Her mouth was against Roi's ear and her words were like warm puffs of air. "Now we're *both* stuck."

"Shhhh." June's proximity was making it hard for Roi to focus.

"How much longer is your shift tonight?" the male voice asked.

"Until ten—or whenever I get these fucking books balanced."

June dropped her chin to Roi's shoulder.

The man laughed. "I feel your pain. It's a zoo up there tonight. See you later."

"Hey, Carl? Call me if you find those receipts from Wednesday night."

Carl's response was unintelligible.

Roi heard the door close and the sounds of Pauline crossing the room and taking her seat at the desk. A drawer opened and closed. Then opened and closed again. The only noise in the room came from papers being shuffled around and occasional, random bursts of typing.

June wasn't moving at all. She still had her chin resting on Roi's shoulder, and she was so still that Roi was half afraid she'd fallen asleep. After a few minutes, they just relaxed into each other. Roi found it more comfortable to stand if she wrapped her arms around June's long body. Having something so soft and solid to hang on to made being stuck in this impossibly prone position easier to contend with. June must have agreed, too, because her own arms eventually wound their tentative way around Roi.

It was actually kind of nice, Roi thought. It was a delicate kind of torture. Like an illicit pleasure—borne of ridiculous circumstances that couldn't possibly have been orchestrated or predicted by either of them. And the darkness made it . . . easier . . . to just stand there in sweet proximity and pretend that none of the feelings she was allowing herself to feel really mattered.

She noticed that June's breathing seemed to be uneven. She could feel every movement of June's chest as it rose and fell against her own.

More time passed. More papers shuffled.

Now Roi's breathing was uneven, too.

June grew still again. So still that Roi softly patted her back, fearing once again that she may have fallen asleep . . . or possibly fearing that she hadn't. It was impossible to know which outcome mattered more. June asleep? June awake? Both? Neither?

In the end, it didn't matter because June *was* awake. June was awake and she had now lifted her head to gently press the side of her face against Roi's.

Roi felt her knees buckle. She tightened her hold on June just to remain standing. But she needn't have worried. June was holding her closer, pushing into her and blowing hot little breaths out against her ear.

Incredible. What was happening was incredible. It was *impossible,* too. The heat that had been rising up between them for days was now pouring out like steam from a Manhattan street vent. It couldn't be put back, it couldn't be stopped, and it couldn't be contained. It had traveled thousands of miles beneath the surface of their painted deserts of disappointed hopes, just to reach this very spot at this precise moment. Roi couldn't think. Couldn't concentrate. Couldn't pay attention to the sounds drifting in from the outer office. She couldn't stop what was happening . . . and she no longer wanted to try.

Everything was beyond their control now. By unspoken

agreement, they'd let go of the reins, and were plunging together into an explosive abyss of raw emotion.

June's fingers were in her hair now, stroking and massaging the back of her head, and moving in light little circles that spiraled down to the center of Roi's being in a whirlpool of longing. She was trapped inside a dizzying and stupefying rush of feeling that she could no more escape than she could flee the room that held them captive.

She felt the soft brush of June's lips against her ear.

Heat. *How could there be so much heat?* Roi was burning up from it. Her skin was hot. Her hands were shaking. Her heart was hammering so hard she was sure the noise it made would give them away. Light flashed behind her eyes. Light that rolled and surged in hot, liquid flashes, illuminating every dark corner of her being and swallowing up all the darkness that surrounded her. That haunted her.

She lifted her head to try and calm herself. To quiet her heart. To try and steady her breathing. *June.* She didn't say the name out loud, but she panted it—pushing the silent anthem out between them on a deep, quiet whisper of air. *June,* she breathed again. This time, June answered her.

The kiss went on and on. So long that Roi was no longer sure where she ended and June began. They were dissolving into each other and all of their carefully constructed barriers were rolling away like the candies that had scattered beneath June's bunk on the train. And all of it was happening quietly. Completely. *Perfectly.*

June's soft, warm hands were holding Roi's face as they continued to explore each other. The air in the closet was thick with the heady aromas of Pine Sol and geranium-scented soaps, but June's sweet, soft bouquet of white peach and ginger overwhelmed it all.

Roi felt herself starting to sway. They were moving more urgently against each other. On some distant level, she knew it was only a matter of time before they knocked something over or failed to suppress their swallowed moans. The telephone in the office rang, and they bolted apart like they'd been doused with cold water.

"What?" Pauline barked.

Roi and June released each other and stood facing each other in the dark. They were both fighting to control their breathing.

"You found them?" Pauline said to whoever was on the line. "Where the hell were they?" A moment later she sighed. "Okay, I'll be right there." She slammed the phone down and pushed back her chair. They heard her leave the office.

Now what?

The seconds ticked by.

"I think she's . . . gone," June whispered.

"Me, too." Roi was still trying to catch her breath.

"We need to get out of here."

"I know."

Roi fumbled for the doorknob with shaking hands. June was right. It was a dud, and they were going no place. She hoped it wasn't an omen for everything they'd just experienced.

"It won't open," she announced.

"I know. Remember? I told you."

Roi sighed. She reached into her jacket pocket and pulled out her wallet.

"What are you doing?" June asked.

"I'm going to try to use a credit card."

She got hold of one of her cards and fumbled for the door again. It was difficult, but she managed to work the card into the side rail above the lock mechanism.

"Here goes," she said. She gave the card a quick, firm downward yank. It got stuck, and the lock didn't budge. "Shit."

"What is it?"

Roi sighed. "Apparently this lock doesn't take American Express."

June actually chuckled. Something about that made Roi feel better.

"Could we just force it?" June asked.

"If we did, we'd tear up the casing. I don't think we'd be able to explain that."

June sighed. Roi felt a hand grab her arm. "Wait. There's a toolbox in here."

"Where?"

"Behind us, on the floor."

"Great." Roi tried to turn around, but she kept running into a wall of nurse. "Okay. We're going to have to do this together."

"Do what together?"

"Turn around." Roi pulled June closer. It was like déjà vu all over again. She noticed that June didn't seem to be protesting. "Let's both take baby steps in a circle to the left. Ready? Go."

They began their conjoined rotation.

"I feel like I'm in an Esther Williams movie," June said.

"Consider it practice for your dance routine."

Roi couldn't see the eye roll that she was fairly sure June made. She bent down and promptly smacked her head on something. "Ow!"

"What happened?" June's hands were on her back.

"I hit my head on the damn handle of something."

"Probably the vacuum cleaner."

Roi was rubbing her head. "Thanks for the warning."

June's hand was moving in small circles between Roi's shoulder blades. "Do you need me to take a look at it?"

Roi had to laugh at the irony. "Sure . . . let me get out my flashlight." As soon as she'd uttered the phrase, she threw her head back and sighed.

"What is it?"

"I'm such an idiot." Roi fumbled inside her jacket again and pulled out her cell phone. She activated its screen and the interior of the closet illuminated with faint, blue light. She held the phone up and rotated her upper body to show June.

"I have a . . ." June's form was glowing in the blue light like an apparition. She reminded Roi of Elvira, the seductive ghost in that Oscar Wilde play. She looked distant and immediate all at the same time. Roi closed her eyes to try to reset her brain. "*Flashlight.* I have a flashlight." She swiped through her various screens until she found the app. She pressed it, and the phone sent out a piercing beam of white light.

Roi waved it along the floor until she saw the toolbox. She bent down—more carefully, this time—and tugged it closer. It had someone's initials inscribed on top. "PLP."

"I think this might be Pauline's," she said.

She opened it. *Shit.* It wasn't a toolbox it was a tackle box. The top tray was divided into about eighteen small compartments, and each of them was filled with various hooks, sinkers, and lures. She lifted the tray out, just in case there might be something like a screwdriver in the bottom well. No such luck. She fanned the phone back and forth over the jumbled contents.

"No dice. It's a tackle box. There's nothing in here but fishing stuff," she said.

"Oh, no. Isn't there anything we can use?"

Roi held up a syringe. "Not unless you can medicate the door into submission."

"Wait. What is that?" June sounded anxious.

"It's some kind of hypodermic needle."

"In a tackle box? What else is in there?"

Roi took a closer look. "Um. Latex gloves, swabs." She picked up a tiny, glass vial. "Some tiny bottles of . . . something."

"Roi." June's voice was practically vibrating with excitement.

"Oh, jeez." Roi felt like an idiot. "This is it, isn't it? This is the stuff used to taint the lip balm."

"Of course it is. It has to be." June bent over and extended a hand. "Give me one of the vials so we can have Bruce test it to be sure."

Roi handed one to June, then closed the box and pushed back into its spot.

"What are you doing?"

"I'm putting it back the way it was. We don't want Pauline to know we found out about this until we're sure she was involved." She stood up. "And that might be the only thing that keeps us safe until we can get out of this damn closet."

"I see your point."

Roi sighed and waved the flashlight around, looking for anything that might be used to jimmy the door.

"Um, Roi?" June asked.

"Yeah?"

"Your phone?"

Roi was now running the beam of light along the top of the utility shelves. "What about it?"

"Could you possibly use it to call someone to come and open the door for us?"

Roi stopped cold. *Fuck.* Her brain must still be on complete tilt from their earlier . . . session. "Oh, god. What a nimrod."

She quickly shut off the flashlight and pulled up her contact list. She scrolled through it until she landed on the number she wanted. Then she held the phone to ear.

"Hi. Fay? It's Roi . . ."

THE CLOSET DOOR finally swung open, and the first thing they saw was Fay, hovering in an explosion of yellow backlight. She was sporting both a martini glass, and an ironic expression.

"I'd say come out of the closet," she said to Roi. "But in your case, I'd be about twenty years too late." She shifted her gaze to June. "You, on the other hand, seem to be running a bit ahead of schedule."

Roi and June stumbled out of the closet and stood together, blinking and shielding their eyes against the light.

"What the hell were you two doing in there?" Fay asked. Then she seemed to think better of it, and held up the palm of her free hand. "Never mind. You can tell me later." She tilted her head toward the club. "We need to get back out there. Poor Smoochie is spread-eagled across your table, trying to keep people from taking the seats. Half the boys in the club think he's a salad bar."

They hurried out of the office, and Roi carefully closed the door behind them. Now that they were back out in the corridor, the music from the club was a lot louder.

"Do you know where Pauline is?" she asked.

"The last time I saw her, she was by the DJ stand, arguing with Bobbie about something."

"She was with Pico?" June asked. "I didn't know they knew each other."

"Oh, they know each other all right. They used to be great friends—college classmates. Bobbie was the reason Pauline moved to Rehoboth."

Roi and June exchanged glances.

"What am I missing here?" Fay asked.

"What?" Roi asked.

They were almost back in the club, and the music was now impossibly loud—ear splitting, actually. It sounded like someone had fallen against the volume control.

A lilting voice rang out and floated above the din.

"I'm . . . coming . . ."

Roi shot a nervous glance at June.

Fay started chuckling.

The siren's call repeated. Roi recognized the voice. Diana Ross.

"I'm coming out."

Fay took June by the arm and escorted her out into the club area where strobe lights were blazing, feet were stomping, glasses were rattling, and six anxious drag queens in full nurse regalia were anxiously casting about for their headliner.

"Okay, doll face." Fay gave June a little push toward the stage. "I think this is your cue."

June shot Roi a panicked look.

Roi straightened her cap.

June gave her a small, grateful-looking smile and handed Roi her cape.

Roi was confused. "Don't you need this?"

"No," she said. "I already know how to fly."

She squared her shoulders and vaulted up the steps to the stage.

The crowd in the club saw her take her place in line with the other "nurses," and the noise they generated completely drowned-out the music—and that should have been an aural impossibility.

"Ladies and gentlemen," a voice on the PA system barked. "It is my privilege to welcome you to The Blue Lagoon. I'm Marianne Unfaithful, and for one night only, I'll be your mistress." She paused and waited while the crowd went wild. "I meant of *ceremonies*. However, if anyone would like to make an offer—I'll need Thursdays off and a good spa membership."

Roi stared up at the unusually tall emcee who was standing on the edge of the stage wielding a cordless microphone. She was wearing white sequins and shoes that probably cost more than Roi made in a month. She had a cascade of dark, curly hair that flowed off her broad shoulders like escaping floodwaters.

Roi gave Fay an enquiring look.

"Another friend of Bobbie's," Fay said. "She makes Miranda Priestly look like Little Nell."

Roi slowly shook her head and took another look at June, who was now happily sandwiched in the center of the "chorus line" between clones of Bette Davis and . . . Bette Midler? It was hard to tell.

"I guess I'd better go to work," she said. "See you after the show?"

"You know it, kid."

Roi made her way to their table and gave a weary thumbs-up to Smoochie, who was on his feet, clapping and whistling.

"Where the hell have you been?" Bruce shouted.

"It's a long story," Roi hollered. "Thanks for watching the stuff . . . I owe you."

She draped June's cape over a chair and took up her camera. She pointed a finger at the stage, and waved at him before beginning her hunt for the best vantage points.

Marianne Unfaithful was still working the crowd.

"And that's the best way I know to get pesky, morning-after stains off your leather bustier."

There were more roars of applause.

Marianne shielded her eyes like she was peering at something near the back of the club. "Oh, my god. Do not even *tell* me you are still wearing that. Honey. We had this conversation already. Friends tell friends, okay? Next Tuesday, it's time to take out the trash."

The laughter was nearly as loud as the music. She warmed to her task.

"Oh, honey? Are you looking for your boyfriend? I just saw Skeletor out in the parking lot, pounding a milkshake and a ham sandwich. That was at least ten minutes ago, so the smart money is on finding him in the bathroom."

More laughter.

"Let's just hope his aim is a tad more specific than the rest of you."

There were a few moans.

"Oh don't give me that . . . As long as you boys hit *something,* you're happy."

Laughter and spirited clapping.

"Okay. Are we ready to get this show on the road?"

Wild rounds of cheering and applause.

"It's now time to meet our Queens of the Night! Ladies and gentlemen. Put your hands together for Rehoboth's own Aquanetta Champüe and Poodle Beach Girls in their all-star tribute to the Angels of Mercy!"

The line of naughty nurses surged forward and took a perfectly synchronized bow.

"And The Blue Lagoon is proud to welcome its very *special* guest, and the inspiration for tonight's show, June Magee, R.N."

Bette Davis and Bette Midler pushed June forward so she could take a solo bow. The cheers and wolf whistles were so loud that Roi half expected the stage lights to shatter.

"That's right, everyone. I think tonight's the night we *really* get to find out what June would do!" Marianne shouted above the applause. "And just in case you weren't sure, here's Miss Diana Ross to remind us that *they're . . . coming . . . out!*"

The club went ape shit. Marianne glided off the stage, the music got louder, and the All Nurse Drag Show commenced.

Roi stood on a chair near the end of the runway and started shooting.

The driving beat of the extended-play, dance remix of the Diana Ross anthem was contagious. Roi had to fight to stay on top of her chair and hold the camera steady.

Each one of the "nurses" took her turn strutting up stage, lip-syncing a verse, busting some moves, and displaying her healing wares to the admiring crowd.

Beneath the neon lights, low-cut, form fitting, tight-skirted white uniforms that had fueled a generation of fantasies flashed like blue fire. The number was hot. Sexy. Sensational. *June* was sensational. She stormed the runway like Grant stormed Richmond—only this conquering hero took *no* prisoners. She owned the place—lock, stock, and tongue depressors.

Her saucy, spirited stage presence mesmerized Roi. It was clear that June was enjoying this . . . and good god . . . could the woman ever *dance.*

"Ooohhh, yeah." The emcee broke in to egg her on. "Get it girl!" She chanted along with the music. "This time around— *she's gonna do it like you never knew it!"*

Roi understood that the photos she was taking would never see the light of day, much less reach the pages of the *Mercury*, but she didn't care. This was a June the world had never seen before, and she was on fire.

*"That's right, everyone. I think tonight's the night
we really get to find out what June would do!"*

It quickly became apparent that Roi wasn't the only one who understood that something extraordinary was happening on stage at The Blue Lagoon. Aquanetta, the big, six-foot-four lead drag queen surged forward and grabbed June by the hand. Almost like they'd rehearsed it a hundred times, the two of them fell into a perfectly executed Latin Hustle. They took over the stage with their rock steps, turns, side breaks, wheels, and wraps. A little bit swing, a little bit salsa, a lotta bit hot—at least it was once Roi was able to embrace the surreal concept that she was watching June tear up the dance floor with another . . . nurse.

The remaining Angels of Mercy dropped back—lip-syncing and cheering the dynamic duo on. They moved and swayed in a curious and exceptionally well-endowed imitation of an eclectic set of Supremes.

Aquanetta released June with a last set of spins and flourishes, and the two of them took their places back in line. The big finale was coming, and it was clear that each of the dancers had a signature move. One by one they twirled, twisted, sashayed, bumped, or sprang into their final poses in the tableaux taking shape at the front of the stage.

With each sequence of moves, the roar of the crowd got louder. June was last to go, and the whole place was clamoring for her to bring it home. Roi had no idea what was left in June's medical bag of tricks, but she was pretty sure it would be impossible for her to top the rest of her show-stopping performance.

June's eyes scanned the crowd and stopped on Roi.

Roi lowered her camera.

There she was again . . . the *other* June. The gentle one who moved on little cat feet, like Carl Sandberg's fog.

The seconds ticked by.

On a cognitive level, Roi understood that the music and the cheering continued to spiral around them on the air inside the club. A few moments ago, it had been so loud in the club that she thought her ears might bleed. But as she stood there atop her small wooden chair looking back at June, the only sound she recognized was the pounding of her own heart.

June smiled.

A nanosecond later, June reached down, grabbed the hem of her dress between both hands, and ripped its side seam halfway to her waist. Then she became a blur.

Roi barely had time to raise her camera before June launched into a perfect cartwheel and landed in a full split—coming to rest dead center between Aquanetta and Pico—just as the last note of music sounded.

The red sole of June's Christian Louboutin Décolleté pump glowed in the stage light.

The crowd stared in a moment of stunned silence before the entire place went berserk.

People were on their feet and rushing the stage. They were going wild and Roi nearly got knocked off her chair.

The Angels of Mercy had hoisted June up and were bearing her off the stage like a champion gladiator.

Roi tried to fight her way through the crowd to reach her, but it was impossible. The crush of admirers was too dense to penetrate. The tall and glittery emcee, however, managed to clear a path through the melee and wrap June up in a one-armed hug. Then she handed her something.

Roi ducked and squinted to get a better look.

Oh shit.

It looked like another glass of that tea.

"ARE YOU SURE I did all right?"

Roi and June were in the tiny elevator at the Sands, and Roi had her hands full trying to keep June upright. It was like a comedy of errors—a ludicrous parody of their earlier encounter in a different closet.

"Yes," Roi said for the tenth time. Or was it the twentieth time? "You were wonderful. Amazing. *Phenomenal.*"

"Really?" June leaned into her. *Fell into her would be more accurate.* "You think so?"

Roi gently pushed her back. "I do. Here." She held up an open water bottle. "Have another sip. We're almost to our room."

"Our room." June giggled. "I like that." She took a sip from the bottle. "I liked that iced tea, too. Do we have any more of it?"

"No, we'd don't. But this water is just as good. Have some more."

"Okay." June complied.

At least she's an agreeable drunk, Roi thought.

June swayed and the navy blue cape slid off her shoulders, exposing most of her right thigh. Her acrobatics on stage had pretty much consigned her dress to the rubbish bin.

Roi groaned. *She's an incredibly hot drunk, too.* She picked up June's cape and resettled it around her shoulders.

June yawned. "I'm so sleepy."

"Me, too," Roi agreed. "Just hang on. You'll be in bed soon."

"Bed." June's voice was dreamy. "Bed is *good.*"

"Yes, it is. Bed is very good."

"Bed with you would be *great.*"

June's hands were wandering again.

Somebody up there fucking hates me. Roi bit her lip and pushed June's hands back to a safe position. "Keep still, now. This is our floor."

The elevator dinged.

"Ding, ding, ding went the bell," June crooned in her soft alto voice.

I don't have a snowball's chance in hell of surviving this, Roi thought.

The door opened, and Roi wrapped an arm around June's shoulders. "Come on. Lean on me. We're almost there."

"I can lean on you," June muttered. "Always."

They made slow progress down the hallway. Roi propped

June up against the wall while she fumbled in her pocket for the key card.

"Open sesame," June commanded. She reached out a hand and laid it flat against Roi's chest. "I danced for you . . . like Salomé. Did you like it?"

Roi looked at her. "I liked it a lot."

June leaned toward her. "You *did?*" Her lips were a hair's breadth away.

Roi nearly let it happen. She *wanted* to let it happen. *Why not?* June was certainly telegraphing her willingness.

But she knew she couldn't. Not this way. Not when it was likely that June wouldn't remember it in the morning. Or if June did remember it, it would be with regret.

No. If it ever happened, Roi wanted it to be something they'd both remember—gladly.

She pulled back and opened the door.

"Come on. Let's get inside."

Roi guided June into the room and turned on a lamp. She dropped the cape and handbag onto a chair.

"Where is your nightgown?" she asked.

"In there." June pointed toward a drawer. "The white one."

Roi opened the drawer. It contained at least five white nightgowns. She sighed and randomly selected one. "Come on." She led June to the bathroom and turned on the light. "Can you get ready for bed by yourself?"

June nodded.

"Good." Roi handed her the nightgown. "Call me if you need me."

June giggled. "What should I call you?"

"Roi will work just fine."

"Okay." June lowered her voice a full octave. "Roi."

Roi was biting the inside of her lip so hard she was sure it would split in half.

"I'll be right outside," she said. She closed the door and walked back into the bedroom.

Good god. Please just make this nightmare end.

She walked across the room to close their sliding door. The winds had picked up and the ocean waves were rolling in with a vengeance. It was clear that the tide wasn't cooperating, either. Nothing would go quietly into this night. She hesitated.

Maybe leaving the door open is a good idea? The sound might lull her into sleep.

Roi pulled the drapes closed and set about turning down June's bed. Then she plopped down into a chair to wait for June's return.

It was taking her a long time. Just when she began to worry that maybe June had fallen asleep, she heard a faint noise. It sounded like . . . tapping.

Three short. Three long. Three short.

Roi closed her eyes. *Not again?*

She got up and walked to the bathroom door.

"June? Are you okay?"

A small voice answered. "The door won't open."

Roi tried the knob. It was locked. She sighed.

"It's locked, June. Undo the latch . . . at the top."

There was a click. The door swung open.

June was standing there with a bewildered expression on her face.

"I did it wrong," she said. She turned her head and grabbed at the fabric on her shoulder. "The front is on the back."

She was in her nightgown, all right, but she'd managed to put it on backwards.

Roi sighed. "We can fix that." She stepped into the bathroom. "Raise your arms over your head."

June obeyed. Roi took hold of the nightgown and pulled it up to try and free her arms, but realized quickly that June wasn't wearing anything beneath it. She yanked it back down immediately and it got stuck on June's head.

"Hey," June complained. "Who turned off the lights?"

Oh, god. Roi felt herself starting to lose it. *There was only so much more of this she could withstand.*

"June? You'll have to do this yourself."

"How?" June flailed her arms around. "I can't see my head."

"Okay, okay." Roi reached out again to stop her frantic movements. "But we're just going to get your arms out *one at a time*. You understand?"

"I think so."

Roi tugged one side of the garment up and helped June successfully extract her arm from the sleeve. They repeated the maneuver on the other side. Once her arms were free, Roi rotated the gown around. The deep V-neck on the front gaped open and left little to the imagination. She swallowed hard and fastened the tiny buttons with shaking hands.

"That's better," June said. "Now my front is right where it's supposed to be."

You can say that again. Roi now had empirical proof that *every* part of June Magee, R.N. was right where it was supposed to be.

"Come on." Roi gently guided her out of the bathroom and turned off the light. "Let's get you into bed."

June leaned heavily against her as they crossed the room. Roi could tell she was starting to drop off. She was nearly dead weight by the time they reached her bed.

"Hang on," Roi said. "Let me pull the covers back."

"Okay." June draped her arms around Roi's neck.

When Roi tried to lower June to the mattress, June held on and pulled Roi right along with her.

Roi tried to push herself up so she wouldn't crush her, but June wouldn't let go of her. The woman was surprisingly strong.

"This is nice," she cooed.

Roi didn't disagree. June was warm and soft. She smelled like white peaches and ginger. They fit together perfectly.

Her face was pressed into June's shoulder. She made another valiant effort to sit up.

"June? June? Let me up. It's time to sleep."

She managed to lift her head so she could look into June's eyes.

June slid her hands from her shoulders to the back of her head. She pulled her down again.

"Marie," she whispered against Roi's mouth.

Roi was losing focus. "What did you say?"

"My name." June kissed her again. "It's Marie."

"Marie?"

June's lips were moving along her collarbone now.

"Yes," she said. "June is a nickname."

"Nickname?" Roi asked. *What was a nickname?* She had no idea what it meant. She had no idea what *anything* meant. Sense and reason were deserting her like rats fleeing a sinking ship.

"I was born in June," she said. Her soft words hummed along Roi's skin, sinking into every hidden part of her. June's hands were moving again, doing amazing things. Rendering Roi too weak to resist even if she'd wanted to. And right now, she didn't want to.

June pulled Roi's face down to hers again. "My father called me his little June Bug."

They were kissing, and Roi groaned when she felt her cell phone ring.

June felt it too. "You're vibrating." She nipped at Roi's nose. "I like it."

The phone vibrated again.

Roi dropped her head to June's chest. "I need to answer it."

June didn't reply, so Roi assumed she agreed.

She pushed herself up into a sitting position and pulled her phone out of her pocket. It was Fay calling.

"Hello?" Roi tried to make her voice sound normal. It wasn't easy.

"Hello, yourself. I wanted to call and make sure you got the goods delivered."

Roi closed her eyes. Fay had no idea how ironic her question was.

"Yeah. We made it back just fine."

"Great. I was thinking that your dancing queen might benefit from a big, greasy breakfast before her talk tomorrow."

"That's probably a good idea," Roi agreed.

"Okay. Meet me at Robinhood Restaurant on Rehoboth Avenue. Bonnie has an early tee time, so it'll be just me. Can you be there by nine o'clock?"

"I think so. We need to fill you in on what we found out tonight, anyway."

"I'll be there with bells on," Fay said. "Which, in my case, is usually mistaken for a fire alarm. I use it as a ruse to get the best table."

Roi laughed. "See you there."

"Righto." Fay hung up.

Roi sat still for a moment, staring at her phone. She owed Fay big time. So did June. The perfectly timed interruption had saved them both from making a huge mistake. There'd have been no going back for them if they'd breached that boundary. And, lord, had it ever been close.

Wonderfully, perfectly, close.

She sighed and angled around to face June, ready to say as much to her. Ready to reassert control and say that things would be a lot clearer for each of them in the morning.

But she didn't have to deliver her well-intentioned speech. June had fallen asleep.

June had fallen asleep, and Roi was left alone to sort out the tangled mess of her emotions.

She got to her feet, pulled the covers up, and tucked them in around June's long, lovely body. She bent down and kissed June on top of her red head.

"Sweet dreams, June Bug," she whispered.

CHAPTER SEVEN
The Morning After

"YOU WANT HOME fries with that feta omelet?" the waitress asked.

June nodded. "And I'd also like a large orange juice. And rye toast—burn it. Oh . . . and a side of turkey bacon, too. Extra crispy."

Roi was staring at her with an open mouth.

"What?" June asked. "Did you want some, too?"

Roi looked at their server. "No. I'll be just fine with the oatmeal."

Fay chuckled and passed her menu over to the waitress. "Just bring me my usual, doll."

"You got it, Fay." She scribbled a few notes on her pad. "Still want that double order of Scrapple for Windsor?"

Fay nodded. "Make it to go—and tell Rocco to get a good scald on it."

"Ten-four." The waitress departed.

"Windsor?" Roi asked.

"My Miniature Schnauzer. He's more of a drama queen than Günter when he doesn't get his way."

June was horrified. "You feed him *Scrapple*?"

"Of course," Fay replied. "He's hypoallergenic, not kosher."

Roi laughed.

June noticed the basket of crackers on their table. "Would you mind passing me some of those Captain's wafers?" she asked Fay. "I'm just so famished."

"She didn't eat much last night," Roi clarified. "I think that show really took it out of her."

"I don't doubt it." Fay passed the crackers to June. "I guess that flying Wallenda routine burns a lot of calories."

"Oh, that." June was embarrassed. "I honestly don't know what came over me. I haven't done a stunt like that since high school."

"Really? Where'd you go to high school? Bratislava?"

Roi choked on her coffee.

"Well, wherever it was, it must be like riding a horse, because you sure looked like a pro." Fay shook her head. "But it's gotta be hell on the shoes—not to mention the uniform."

"I think I was just . . . caught up in the moment." June didn't dare look at Roi. "The atmosphere in there is pretty infectious."

"Tell me about it. The atmosphere at MIXX is infectious, too. But for some reason, the only part of me that ever gets infected is my liver."

June smiled at her. "I think I know what you mean. I had a few too many of those iced tea concoctions last night. I'm lucky I didn't lose control altogether."

"You had *a few* of the Lagoon's iced teas?" Fay was incredulous. "Honey. Forget about nearly losing control. You're lucky you didn't wake up in Tijuana with a Chihuahua and a butt load of tattoos."

"Oh, Fay." June lowered her eyes. "I wasn't *that* far gone." She cast an appealing look at Roi. "Was I?"

Roi seemed uncomfortable with the question. "You were still . . . yourself. Mostly."

Mostly? Now June was truly mortified. *That whole closet scenario had been bad enough. She was horrified by the memory of her forwardness and her unguarded behavior. What must Roi think of her? And what on earth had she done when they got back to the hotel? And how had Roi reacted?*

She was too terrified to even speculate.

"I'm glad," she said. She tried to make her voice as neutral sounding as possible. "I'd be terribly upset if I thought I had done anything to make anyone . . . uneasy."

Roi didn't say anything, but June could tell by her expression that uneasy was exactly the way this conversation was making her feel. She resolved to change the topic. Quickly.

"So I need to fill you both in on what I overheard when I was locked in the closet."

Roi raised an eyebrow.

"The *first* time," June clarified.

Fay chuckled.

"Pauline came into the office, and she was with someone. A man. I think she called him Alphonse."

"Alphonse?" Fay leaned forward. "Alphonse from Chester, Alphonse?"

"I think that's right," June said.

Fay tsked. "That's not good news."

"It didn't sound like it. I gathered that Pauline had enlisted his services for something that had gone horribly wrong, and that she was very concerned about finding a way to correct the situation."

"Wait a minute." Roi leaned toward her. "You think Pauline got the chemicals used to taint the lip balm from this Alphonse character?"

June nodded. "That's what it sounded like to me, yes."

Fay appeared unconvinced. "I just can't believe that. Pauline is a tough cookie, but I can't imagine she'd ever do something like this."

"That's just it," June explained. "I don't think she ever intended for it to go this far. Alphonse said something about her wanting to make a statement. I honestly think that's all it was. She seemed sincere about wanting to find a way to make things right."

"Make a statement?" Fay waved a hand in obvious frustration. "Who makes a statement by giving women poison ivy on their hoo-has?"

"*Symptoms* of poison ivy," Roi clarified. "Not the real thing."

"Right," June added. "Just enough of a case to make them uncomfortable."

"And to ruin Women's FEST. That's the part I just don't

get. Not from Pauline." Fay shook her head. "Besides, she's one of our best volunteers."

"I'll admit that this is the one part that doesn't make sense to me either." June thought about it. Something else occurred to her. "Unless . . ."

Roi and Fay exchanged glances.

"Unless . . . what?" Roi asked.

"There was something Alphonse said to Pauline when they were arguing. Something about getting help next time from her Gamma Rho sisters—if any of them would still talk to her."

"Gamma Rho?" Fay asked.

June nodded.

"That's a lesbyterian sorority."

"Pauline was in Gamma Rho?" Roi asked.

"Apparently. Pauline suggested that she was expelled from college for something she didn't do—something related to the theft of some laboratory equipment? I gather that no one stood up for her—including her sorority sisters."

Fay nodded. "That's right. Bobbie and Pauline were undergrad classmates at Rutgers. He said she'd fallen on hard times and needed help finding a job. He was the one who convinced her to come to Rehoboth, probably because he thought she could find an accepting community here. I hooked her up with contacts at The Sands and The Blue Lagoon."

"I don't get it." Roi seemed perplexed. "There doesn't seem to be much love lost between Bobbie and Pauline right now."

"True," Fay agreed. "They had some kind of falling out. I think it happened about the time Pauline started growing the horn." She tapped her forehead.

"You mean she hasn't always had it?" Roi asked.

"No. It only started showing up about several months ago. Her personality has taken a real nosedive since then. Not that she was any Little Miss Sunshine before it appeared."

"I'm certain the affliction hasn't helped with Pauline's anger management issues," June observed. "And it's also true that stress and anxiety are known contributors to the development and progression of her condition. And that's sad, because it's very treatable."

Fay nodded. "Pauline works all the time—but, unfortunately, she only has a bunch of part-time jobs. I don't imagine she can afford any kind of health insurance. I figure that's probably the reason why she hasn't been able to do anything about it before now."

"Sheesh." Roi flopped back against the booth. "What a colossal mess."

June looked at her. She was tempted to say that Roi's pronouncement was true on a *lot* of levels, but she kept silent.

"Well, what do we do now?" Fay asked.

"We can't prove anything until Bruce gets back to us with the test results on that vial we found in Pauline's tackle box." Roi finished her cup of coffee.

June was surprised. "You gave that to Bruce?"

Roi nodded. "Before we left the club last night. I also filled Fay in on what we found." She paused. "I guess you don't remember?"

"I confess that I don't remember much of anything that happened last night."

Roi didn't respond. June couldn't tell if the expression on her face was one of relief or disappointment.

Fay tapped her fingers against the side of her water glass. She looked like she wanted to say something. June decided to step into the void.

"I've never been much of a drinker," she explained. "I apologize if I behaved in any ways that were . . . unseemly."

"Oh, honey. There was nothing unseemly about anything you did last night." Fay cut her eyes to Roi. "At least nothing that I know anything about. Besides, I believe that anyone who can drink more than one of The Lagoon's iced teas and still have a functioning brain stem should donate their metabolism to science."

Roi laughed, and for some reason, that made June feel less anxious.

"I'm still horrified with myself. Believe me when I tell you that last night was not . . . normal . . . behavior for me."

Fay—on the opposite side of the booth–quietly regarding June and Roi. It went on for so long that June started to feel antsy—like the two of them had been called into the principal's office and were about to be reprimanded for something.

"Of course, I can only speak for myself, but I think what the two of you need is a whole lot more *abnormal* behavior." She shook her head. "You should consider getting locked in closets more often. Maybe it would help you figure things out."

June was relieved that their waitress chose that moment to show up with the coffee pot. It saved her from making any immediate reply. Besides, she was sure that whatever she said would just dig her in deeper.

Roi made a subtle shift away from her in the booth. June couldn't tell if the movement was anecdotal or purposeful. All she knew was that she missed the subtle pressure of Roi's arm against hers.

"I think one outing in a storage closet is enough for us," Roi said. She looked at June. "I think we do better work in the daylight, where things are clearer."

June gave her a small, grateful smile. Roi was letting her off the hook, and June knew it. This was precisely the outcome she thought she wanted. She sincerely hoped that, in time, getting what she wanted would feel better than it did right now.

Fay, however, didn't appear to be buying it.

"Life is short," she said. "Bonnie and I have learned this lesson the hard way. When the universe throws you a curve ball, you have to step right up and swing for the fences. You never know when you'll get lucky and make that connection. And when you do? When you step out with a little faith and a lotta guts, and that ball sails right out of the park? It's magic."

June was too embarrassed and afraid to make any reply. Roi was silent, too.

"Okay," Fay added, after an uncomfortable silence. "So, clearly, I suck at baseball analogies."

Roi smiled. "No. We just have better sense than to swing at a wild pitch."

"Smart ass." Fay shook her head. "I knew I liked you, kid."

THE AUDITORIUM AT CAMP Rehoboth was packed with people. Roi was pretty sure that many of the faces she was seeing this morning belonged to revelers who had been in the club last night. She also recognized many of the people who had attended the bookstore readings, including several of the authors. But nothing surprised her more than seeing Pauline Polito slink in and lay claim to one of the last, empty seats at the back of the hall. To say that June's talk today was drawing a mixed crowd was definitely an understatement.

It looked to her like today's male-to-female ratio was about fifty-fifty. Not at all surprising after the performance last night. June had all but solidified her reputation as a gay icon. And why not? After all, she was a drag queen's fantasy.

Hell, she'd be a viable fantasy for anyone with a pulse.

Including me, Roi thought.

But it was best not to spend any more time wandering down that garden path. It had shaped up to be nothing more than an endless maze of twists and turns that didn't lead anywhere. June had made that much clear at breakfast this morning. Once this assignment was over, they'd go their separate ways and Roi would do her best to put everything that did and didn't happen between them into a box and file it away on the back shelf of her subconscious with the rest of her bad relationship choices. She could do that. She had lots of experience at it.

She knew better. Allowing herself to become attracted to a straight woman was an insane and losing proposition. She blamed their aberrant behavior on the unusual circumstances of their whirlwind, three-day cohabitation and the surreal venue that served as the backdrop for this assignment. She could understand how they could fall prey to lapses in judgment that they now chose to regret.

At least, June appeared to regret *her* lapses in judgment. Roi really had no choice but to respect that outcome, and to find a way to move forward that wouldn't embarrass either of them or compromise any future working relationship they might end up having. Max was enough of a sadistic bastard that it was easy to imagine he'd continue to assign Roi to cover at least some of June's future appearances. And that would be especially true once he got a gander at some of the shots Roi had been able to snag during this venture. Putting all modesty aside: they were phenomenal. Pure and simple. But when she had a subject the camera loved like it loved June Magee, no outcome short of phenomenal would really be possible.

Still . . . Roi was irrationally pleased at how well the chronicle of images had come together. Too bad she'd never be able to include any of the June Unplugged shots from last night's performance at The Blue Lagoon. Those would forever be consigned to her private collection . . . just like the memories of everything else that had transpired between them.

The ambient chattering in the room fell silent. Fay Jacobs had stepped up to the podium, and she was beginning her introduction.

Roi could see June just offstage. She looked composed and perfectly put together. Just as she had looked the first time Roi had met her. It was amazing. Even last night, when she was splayed out across the stage floor in a full split, she exuded calm and ease—as if ripping her dress nearly in half and launching herself into a cartwheel in front of a couple hundred strangers was an everyday occurrence.

You couldn't fake a demeanor like that. You had to be born to it.

While Fay continued with her remarks, June waited patiently in a hallway, standing just in front of a card rack that was loaded with dozens of brightly colored brochures. They were displayed alongside announcements, newsletters, and various invitations to benefits and potluck suppers. All the things one would expect to see in a small town community center. A stray breeze blew in from someplace, and it caused the backdrop of papers to shift and flutter like dry leaves.

Roi raised her camera and framed June, looking pensive and self-possessed, before a wall of moving words. It was a fantastic metaphor—an image that resonated with the force of a hundred subliminal messages.

Snap.

Before she could steal a second shot, Fay finished her introduction.

June walked out to join her on the small stage. Roi was surprised that she wasn't carrying any of the note cards she'd spent part of the morning reviewing.

The clapping and cheering in the hall went on and on. June had clearly staked her claim in the collective heart of this diverse community.

Roi had never heard June deliver one of what Max called her stump speeches. The reading in the bookstore yesterday had been just that: a reading. But today was different. Today, June Magee had something to say—and it looked like she was going to waste no time getting down to saying it.

"It's an honor for me to be here with all of you today. Any of you who had the grave misfortune to witness my uncer-emonious debut as an eclectic Angel of Mercy last night will, I hope, forgive the lack of propriety. Please do not infer from this appearance that I have either the inclination or the talent to pursue a career in show business. I assure you that I do not."

There was a hearty round of laughter.

"I would also observe," June continued, "that any such career aspirations would seem to require a wardrobe allowance that eludes me at present. And before I leave here today, I'd like to ask if any of you in the audience could be so kind as to refer me to a competent seamstress?"

The audience laughed and offered up some spirited applause. A couple of hands shot into the air.

"But, in all seriousness," June continued. "I confess that when I first learned that I'd be privileged to attend this festival, I knew very little about its uniqueness. I'd never been to Rehoboth Beach before, and I'd certainly never heard of a unique place called CAMP Rehoboth. "What would June do in circumstances like these?"

A few people in the audience shouted out replies. June smiled at them good-naturedly.

"No, no . . . this isn't a quiz. Not *yet,* anyway."

Laughter.

"Shall I tell you what June would do?"

Energetic head nods all around.

"June would do diligence. June would do research. June would do her homework." She paused. "June would also encourage you not to be terrified of someone who refers to herself in the third person."

Laughter.

"But the most important thing June would do is pay attention." She paused and gazed at her audience. "You know, the great entertainer Barbra Streisand once quipped that she didn't care what people said about her as long as they spelled her name *wrong.* In a similar vein, I don't care what people say about *June* as long as they acknowledge that she paid attention."

Roi lowered her camera. *She did not just play the Barbra Streisand card?* She looked back at the audience. They were mesmerized. This woman was a fucking genius.

"Paying attention isn't just about noticing things like the color your hotel is painted, the location of the lifeguard stands, or the time left on any of the ubiquitous parking meters that line the avenues of this wonderfully quirky town.

"Paying attention means learning to see the world around you with a different set of eyes. It means looking beyond what lies on the surface and listening to what hides behind the sounds.

"Paying attention is one of the least—and most—scientific things we can do.

June Magee, R.N.

"I am reminded of a passage I first heard many years ago, in Mrs. Gustafson's Sunday school class at the Dairyland Lutheran Church." June paused, and gave the audience a wry smile. "The fact that I still remember this is more a testament to Mrs. Gustafson's . . . *sturdiness*, than it is any indication of piety."

"'And, behold,' June quoted. "'The Lord passed by, and a great and strong wind rent the mountains, and brake in pieces the rocks before the Lord; but the Lord was not in the wind: and after the wind an earthquake; but the Lord was not in the earthquake: And after the earthquake a fire; but the Lord was not in the fire: and after the fire *a still small voice.*'

"So it is the case that truth and meaning are to be found not in the roar of a hurricane or the shifting of the earth. Not in the rumble of thunder or the heat of a fire. Truth and meaning wait for us in the quiet spaces that divide day from night, hope from longing, faith from reason, and compassion from fear.

"When we pay attention, we open ourselves to a world that resonates with a thousand still, small voices. They surround us. They embrace us. They *improve* us. Together, they spiral upward in a grand chorus of truth, meaning, love, and acceptance.

"When we pay attention, when we listen, when we hear with better ears and see with better eyes, we allow ourselves to embrace a world that is greater than the one we knew. We learn to know each other, even as we are known. We learn to love each other in ways that pass all understanding. And we learn that to forgive is to embrace the best and noblest part of our shared humanity.

"So I shall ask the question again. What would June do? June would pay attention.

"And in so doing, she would learn that these are just a few of the things that define life in an intentional community, where our differences are celebrated, and love and acceptance are our greatest common denominators.

"And she would learn that all of this happens in a remarkable place called CAMP Rehoboth.

"Thank you very much for welcoming me. I'd be honored to take your questions."

For about five seconds, you could have heard a pin drop inside the hall. Then the entire place erupted in thunderous applause. The crowd got to its feet, stomping and cheering. Cell phones were flashing. People were tossing things at the stage. One of the items went astray and landed on Roi. She plucked it off the sleeve of her jacket. It was a tongue depressor.

Another flat projectile sailed past and landed near her foot. This one looked . . . smaller. Roi bent down and picked it up.

It was an Emery board.

I guess that makes sense, she thought. *This place is full of drag queens.*

June was still smiling and waving at the crowd. She let the celebration go on for a minute or so, and then held up her hands to quiet the applause and allow the Q&A portion of her talk to commence.

Hands shot up all over the room.

Roi sighed and decided to look around for an empty seat. She noticed Pauline standing near the courtyard exit— staring right at her. In fact, it felt more like she was staring right *through* her. Roi raised a hand and gave her a small wave. Pauline didn't react. She turned on her heel and left the hall.

That woman is one conflicted, hot mess.

Up on stage, June was responding to a question about whether the rumors were true that she'd soon be replacing Nicolle Wallace on *The View*.

Roi rolled her eyes and sat down. They were going to be here for a while.

THE MEET-N-GREET session in the CAMP courtyard was winding down.

Thank goodness.

June enjoyed these public appearances and the opportunities they presented for interaction with diverse groups of people, but today her stamina for the effort was waning. She knew that a big part of that was a carryover from her night of . . . dissipation. But the rest derived entirely from her anxiety about what had transpired with Roi—both in the storage closet at the club, and later, when they got back to their hotel room.

To be fair, she truly didn't remember all of what took place after they left the club. But she recalled enough to know that Roi had done a yeoman's job getting her back to the hotel and managing her . . . lack of inhibition . . . as she put her to bed.

It was that last part that filled her with trepidation. How far had she actually gone, and how had Roi reacted? Roi's guarded comments this morning at breakfast indicated that she was more than eager to move beyond the experience of whatever had taken place between them last night. June knew she should be grateful for that, but instead, she just felt . . . sad. Disappointed. As though she knew she'd missed out on something extraordinary, but would never really understand what. Or why.

In retrospect, if she were to be honest with herself, she'd be forced to admit that a large part of her anxiety was tied directly to Roi's gender. It would be a lie for June to profess that she'd never been attracted to another woman before. She understood that much about herself, and she accepted it in the same way she accepted that eating shellfish gave her hives. As long as she avoided exposure to the stimulant, she could avoid suffering the consequences of the response. She never regarded her sporadic inclinations as anything other than that: sporadic. She accepted them as an honest and understandable, heretofore minor, part of having a normal and healthy libido.

Of course, her neighbor, Letty, understood this aspect of June's character, too. And that understanding formed part of the basis of their friendship. Letty liked nothing better than to tease June about her presumed and oft-cited prudishness. June was hardly asexual, and Letty knew that. But Letty also knew that June lived her life to avoid complications.

Giving in to her undeniable attraction to Roi was a complication of the first order. It was extremely unusual behavior for her. How did Fay characterize it? Swinging at a curve ball? Well, this time, June certainly chose to take her turn at bat. And her later discovery that Roi was not a man was not just complicated: it was calamitous.

She wasn't ready for this level of disruption. She wasn't prepared for it. All the uncertainties it generated were too great for her to take on right now. They would cause her to lose focus. They were *already* causing her to lose focus. She couldn't afford to derail her emotional stability this way. Not now. Not when she was in a position to do so much good. Her work had to come first—just like it always had.

Things would be clearer when they were back in Chicago. Once they returned to their familiar lives and settled back into their everyday routines, this dense fog of confused intimacy that now surrounded them would lift. Would dissipate. Would be replaced by reason and clarity. Things would make sense again. The unfamiliar terrain they'd been fumbling across would give way to landscapes they both recognized and understood how to safely navigate.

June could return to her ordered life, and Roi could return to whatever defined her own version of normalcy.

The last few attendees gave June their thanks, snapped up their autographed copies of her book, and hurried out the courtyard. It was early afternoon, and the sun was shining. June suspected that all the restaurants in town that offered outdoor seating were already humming with activity.

Roi must have had the same idea. She approached the table where June was still seated.

"Fay says that the chicken salad at this Lori's Café is to die for." Roi jerked a thumb over her shoulder to indicate the small eatery that sat across the courtyard from the entrance to CAMP

Rehoboth. "How about we rustle up a couple of sandwiches and enjoy this warm weather?"

June smiled up at her. "I know it seems that after that breakfast I ate, I wouldn't need food for a week. But to tell the truth, I'm famished."

"You should be." Roi held up her watch. "Breakfast was nearly four hours ago."

"Really?" June was shocked.

"Really. We've got about ninety minutes until your next gig at the convention center."

June sagged against her chair. "I forgot about that."

"I wouldn't worry too much about it. As great as this weather is, I suspect that most people are going to be outside soaking up some sun. All you have to do is walk through and make nice with some of the vendors."

"Make nice? Right now that sounds like a labor of Hercules."

"For you?" Roi shook her head. "Nah. It's like walking a straight line."

Roi's simple analogy reminded June of her undignified deportment last night.

"Not the best choice of metaphor, I fear," she said, apologetically.

Roi rolled her eyes. "Will you lighten up? It's a gorgeous day, and in just about two hours, we'll both be free to do whatever we want."

For some reason, Roi's observation didn't make June feel any better. But she did her best to put up a brave front.

"Okay. Of course you're right." She got to her feet. "I need to duck inside and use the restroom, so how about I meet you back out here in just a few minutes?"

"Sure. Fay's going to join us. I'll go ahead and get the food. What do you want to drink?"

June gave her an ironic look.

"Right," Roi said. "That would be one large water."

June smiled at her and headed for the community center.

When she emerged from the restroom a few minutes later, she was surprised to see Pauline Polito standing outside the door.

"I need to talk to you," Pauline said without preamble. "In private."

June felt a twinge of anxiety, but something about Pauline's expression put her halfway at ease. For the first time, the woman didn't look angry or annoyed. If anything, she looked worried.

"Of course," June said. "When would you like to talk?"

"Now," Pauline answered quickly.

"All right. I have a few minutes." June remembered passing a small kitchen on her way to the restroom. She pointed toward its entrance. "How about we go in there and sit down?"

Pauline nodded and led the way. Once they were both inside, she closed the door and leaned against it. She was wearing her customary red ball cap, and the overhead light in the room caused its overlarge bill to cast deep shadows across most of her face.

"You know it was me, don't you?" Her tone was accusatory.

June was stunned by her question and uncertain about how to respond.

She tried to buy herself some time to think. "I'm not sure I understand what you're asking."

"The lip balm. The rashes. You *know* I'm the one who did it. I *know* you know."

"What makes you think that?" June asked. She had a momentary sense of panic.

Pauline reached into a front pocket and pulled something out. "Here." She extended her hand. "Your little friend left these behind."

June reluctantly took the items from her. Her breath caught when she realized that Pauline had just handed her the two halves of Roi's American Express Card.

"It didn't take a rocket scientist to connect the dots," Pauline said. "She was hiding in the closet, wasn't she?"

"No," June said. "I was."

"*You* were?"

June nodded. "We'd already been able to deduce that the lip balm was the source of the widespread rashes afflicting the festival goers. It seemed likely that someone at The Blue Lagoon had to be involved, but we didn't know whom. I was snooping around the office looking for clues, and when you came back, I hid in the storage closet."

"Oh, my god. And you got stuck?"

June nodded.

"So you used your girlfriend's credit card to try to open the door?"

June's mortification was increasing. "Not exactly. By then, Roi was in the closet with me."

Pauline actually laughed. "You two are like Snooki and JWoww."

June had no idea who they were, but she was pretty sure the comparison wasn't a compliment. She made no reply.

"So what all did you overhear?" Pauline asked.

"It doesn't matter. I heard enough to know that you were having some serious misgivings about the way things turned out."

"Alphonse. *That bastard.*" She looked at June with narrowed eyes. "You heard all of that, didn't you?"

June nodded.

"That speech. Those comments you made." Pauline practically spat out the words. "I was *out* there. You *saw* me out there. You were talking to me, weren't you?"

June knew it was pointless to pretend. They were already well beyond that point. She walked to a small table and pulled out a chair.

"Let's sit down," she said.

To her amazement, Pauline complied.

"Yes," June began. "I did see you. And I was glad to see you. And I do confess that some of my comments *were* intended for you. But not just for you."

Pauline was staring at her with an odd expression.

"Tell me why you did it." June had no idea where her bravado was coming from.

"What *difference* does it make?" Pauline hissed.

"It makes all the difference."

"No it doesn't," Pauline said with bitterness. "Once it comes out, all anyone will care about is that I had an epic fuck up. *Again*. And for once, it really will be my fault."

"Why do you call it a fuck up?" June hesitated. "Was it a mistake?"

"*Yes*." Pauline rubbed a hand across her face. "No. I mean, not *all* of it." She looked at June. "I meant to do it. I meant to stick it to those self-righteous bitches. They *asked* for it. But you have to believe me . . . I never thought it would be a serious thing. I never thought it would hurt anybody." She looked down at the tabletop. "Once I realized it had gone too far, it was too late to stop it."

"Why do you say they asked for it?"

Pauline gave a bitter-sounding laugh. "After what happened to me at Rutgers, I lost everything. My scholarship. My friends. *My freedom*. I did time for something I had nothing to do with. When I got out, I came here for all those lofty reasons you rattled off in your little speech. And for a while, I thought this place and these people might really be different." She yanked off her cap. "But once *this* started," she pointed at the growth near her hairline, "they made it clear that I was nothing but a freak."

"You're not a freak, Pauline."

"Really? Why don't you tell that to all those pampered, trust fund LUGS who roar down here on their spring breaks and live the high life on daddy's credit cards?"

"LUGS?" June was confused.

"Lesbians Until Graduation. They make me sick."

"Pauline?" June waited until Pauline met her eyes. "You're not a freak."

"Says you."

"Says anyone. You certainly aren't the first person to have this condition. And you're not the first person to be rejected or disappointed by people who ought to know better."

"*Right.* Like you'd know anything about rejection."

"I happen to know a lot about rejection. I also know what it feels like to make a wrong turn, and live forever with its consequences."

Pauline snorted.

"I had my own brush with disappointment and betrayal, Pauline. Only mine came at the hands of a third-year resident who swore he loved me, and convinced me we'd be married as soon as he finished his surgical rotation. When I told him I was pregnant, he left me with nothing but a stack of regrets, and the name of a colleague who could handle the problem for me."

Pauline was looking at June with amazement. "I'm . . . What did you do?"

"I had the abortion. And it took me years to learn how to put my life back together and begin the slow process of forgiving myself. But my performance is still imperfect, at best, and I'll always be a work in progress."

"Does anyone else know about this?"

"Not until now."

Pauline shook her head. "Why would you tell me something like this? I could ruin your reputation."

"Yes, you could. But you won't."

"What makes you so sure?"

"Because I trust you. In the same way you can trust me."

Pauline didn't reply.

"Pauline?" June reached across the table and laid a hand on her arm. "Let me help you."

"No one can help me."

"You're wrong."

"Really?" Pauline stood up and waved her arms in frustration. "What are you gonna do, Nurse Magee? Whip out your X-Acto knife and lop it off?"

June sighed. "No. But it is a fairly simple medical procedure that can be handled in an office visit. I can take you to someone who can remove it—safely and discreetly."

"I can't pay for that."

"You won't have to pay for it, Pauline."

"Who will, then? You? I won't take charity."

"It's not charity when it comes from a true friend."

"I don't have any friends. Not any more."

"You're wrong."

Pauline dropped back into her chair. "I burned all those bridges when I spiked the lip balm. Nobody here will help me, now."

"I guess you'll have to take that up with Fay. But if I were you, I wouldn't count on winning. She seems to like getting her way."

"What are you talking about?"

"Fay has a doctor friend who has agreed to do the procedure for you, if you're willing. Gratis."

Pauline started to protest, but couldn't seem to get the words out.

"She knows what happened," June said. "But she understands, and she wants to help you."

"Why?"

"Because, against all reason, there actually are people in the world who understand what it means to be human. And, by loving example, they teach us *every day,* that forgiveness is a power greater than resentment."

"She isn't going to turn me in?"

"No. And neither am I."

Pauline raised a hand to her forehead and touched the skin at her hairline. June saw her fingers shake.

"I don't know what to do," she said. Her voice was smaller.

"Lucky for you, I've spent most of my adult life learning how to help people navigate that very problem."

"I can't undo the past. I can't change what I did."

"No," June agreed. "You're right. What you did was wrong, and it could have had horrible consequences for a lot of people, including yourself. We're all very lucky that it didn't turn out that way. But make no mistake, Pauline. You have a lot of fences to mend, and you need professional help to find better ways to manage your anger and disappointment."

"I can't afford a shrink."

"I understand that. But I'm sure that CAMP Rehoboth has the resources to point you in the right direction."

Pauline didn't reply.

June hoped that meant she'd finally run out of arguments.

"Come on." She stood up and extended a hand. "Let's go meet Fay and have some lunch. Then the two of you can talk about next steps, and where you go from here."

Pauline hesitated only a moment before she slowly got to her feet, and took hold of June's hand.

"I STILL CAN'T believe that happened."

Roi and June were walking along the boardwalk. All the lamppost lights were coming on. They glowed against the blue-black sky like fireflies. The air was starting to cool off, but it was still pleasant. A mild breeze was blowing in off the Atlantic. Parties and celebrations were taking place at venues all over town tonight, but they decided to beg off and enjoy a bit of quiet on their last evening. Besides, Roi had an early flight back to Chicago, and June's train was departing the 30th Street Station several hours later.

June looked at her. "I know. It all came together so quickly. I'm just relieved that Fay was able to pick up the ball and run with it."

"It wasn't hard to tell that something was really different about Pauline's demeanor. Fay noticed the two of you coming out of CAMP right away."

"She did?"

Roi nodded. "You'd been gone for so long that I was about

ready to come looking for you. I was afraid maybe you'd managed to get locked inside another closet."

June threw her head back. "Heaven forefend."

"Hey? At least I was prepared for it this time."

"You were?"

"Uh huh." Roi reached into a pocket on her jacket. "See?" She held up a shiny plastic rectangle.

"Is that a VISA card?"

"Yep. I have it on good authority that most locks in this town accept it."

June rolled her eyes. "You're nuts."

"If you doubt me, we can always test my hypothesis."

"I don't think so."

Roi chuckled.

"By the way." June reached into her cape and pulled out the two broken pieces of Roi's American Express card. "Pauline found these on the floor of the storage closet."

"Oh, god." Roi took them from her. "I realized this morning that somebody would find them. I hoped it wouldn't be Pauline."

"Well, it was. That's how she put two and two together."

"And got five?"

"Not exactly. She thought you were the one who overheard her with Alphonse. Naturally, she assumed that you would tell me everything."

"Naturally."

"And then she figured that my remarks this morning were all intended for her."

"About that . . ." Roi stopped and faced June. "When did you decide to chuck your normal presentation and go rogue?"

June shrugged. "I saw Pauline come into the hall when I was waiting backstage. I figured nothing ventured, nothing gained."

"Well, it was one helluva speech."

June seemed embarrassed. "Really?"

"Yeah, really. You could've sold a shit load of Amway products."

"Very funny."

They resumed walking.

"I'm actually not kidding, June," Roi continued. "It was a pretty incredible speech. I can understand why it resonated for Pauline."

"I'm not sure how much resonance *she* felt it had. She certainly wasn't contrite when she ambushed me outside the restroom."

"I feel terrible about that. I should've listened to my gut and come in there to find you."

"No." June touched Roi's arm. "It happened exactly the way it should have. I think she was relieved that we knew."

"I bet she was a whole lot more relieved to find out that nobody was going to press charges."

"Roi . . ."

"I'm sorry, June. But what she did was contemptible. People could really have been hurt—and for no better reason than because she got dissed by some selfish brats. That's not healthy and it's not okay."

"I agree. And Fay agrees, too. It's going to be a long road for Pauline, and she isn't getting a pass by any stretch of the imagination. Although I do believe that having the cutaneous growth removed will do wonders to improve her attitude."

Roi regretted her outburst. "I don't mean to come across like an uncaring asshole. I know she's had a tough time."

"I know. Your anger is understandable."

"What about yours?"

"What about my what?"

"Your anger. You're a healthcare professional. You must feel some, too."

"Of course I do. But I learned a long time ago that I function better and feel better when I channel my energy and my emotions into looking for positive outcomes."

"You mean like lighting a candle instead of cursing the darkness?"

"Precisely."

"Oprah was right." Roi shook her head. "You really are the Eleanor Roosevelt of medicine."

"I wouldn't go that far."

"Really?" Roi bumped into her playfully. "How far *would* you go?"

"I think you already know the answer to that question."

Roi looked at her. "No. Not really." She gave June a small smile. "But I wish I did."

June slowly shook her head. "I don't know what to say."

They reached the plaza at Rehoboth Avenue. Dolle's was still open. Roi got an idea.

"What kind of popcorn goes with cognac?"

June raised an eyebrow. "Is this an academic question?"

"Nope." Roi shifted her backpack around so she could unzip it. She pulled out their half-full bottle of Remy Martin. "I thought we might find a nice spot on the beach and enjoy a glass of this. I think we earned it today."

June seemed surprised. "That's why you brought the bag along? I thought your camera was in there."

Roi shook her head. "No cameras tonight. Work is over."

June nodded but didn't say anything. She stood looking out at the ocean. The light was fading fast, and the tide was just starting to turn.

Roi began to worry that she'd gone too far, yet again. "June?"

"Cheddar," June said.

"Excuse me?"

"The popcorn." June met her eyes. "White cheddar."

Roi smiled and handed her the backpack. "I've got a towel in here, too. Go pull up some sand. I'll be right back."

June complied and headed toward the steps that led down to the beach.

Roi only took a few minutes to procure the bag of popcorn and rejoin her.

The beach towel Roi had borrowed from the hotel wasn't really large enough to accommodate both of them, so they ended up sitting on June's cape. Roi lent June her jacket so she wouldn't get cold.

The night was clear and the stars were out in droves.

"Look at that star." June pointed toward a bright flare of light that sat low on the horizon.

"That's not a star," Roi corrected. "It's a planet. Jupiter, I think."

"Really?" June looked at her. "Are you sure?"

"Pretty sure. Jupiter's orbit is directly opposite the sun in this sky. So it's the brightest spot in the heavens this time of year. If we sat out here long enough, we'd eventually be able to see some of the brownish cloud belts that make the planet look striped."

June seemed impressed. "How do you know that?"

"Believe it or not, I minored in astronomy. I grew up in the Great Smokey Mountains . . . remember? Star gazing was a big part of my childhood."

"We had beautiful night skies in Wisconsin, too. I miss that."

"Me, too. Whenever I can, I head up to Illinois Beach in Zion, just so I can get away from all the city lights and really see the stars."

"Zion? Isn't that pretty far north?"

"About an hour. Not too bad a drive—and totally worth it to get a dark sky. Plus they don't close it down at eleven, like they do the beaches in Chicago."

"I'd love to see that." June sounded like she really meant it.

"Then I'll have to take you there."

June looked at her in surprise. "Would you really do that?"

"Will you bring the popcorn?"

June smiled. "If you bring the cognac."

Roi held up her plastic cup. "It's a date."

They clinked cups.

June fixed her gaze back on the night sky. "So what else are we seeing tonight?"

"Let's see." Roi took a closer look. "Okay. See the moon out there, riding low on the sky? We should soon see Saturn and Pollux. And up there . . ." She pointed at a cluster of stars. "That's the constellation Pleiades—also called The Seven Sisters."

"Where?" June squinted. "I don't think I've ever seen that one before."

Roi chuckled. "Trust me, you've seen it. Especially *this* weekend."

"What do you mean?"

"It's the symbol on the front of every Subaru."

June rolled her eyes. "Be serious."

"I *am* being serious. It's the term the Japanese use for Pleiades." Roi pointed again. "Look again. Right up there. A cluster of stars, just north of Taurus."

"Taurus?"

"The Bull. Hang on." Roi shifted around behind June so she could extend an arm over her shoulder, close to her head. "Follow my hand. See those three stars in a row?"

June nodded, and her hair brushed against Roi's face.

Roi took a deep breath. "That's Orion's Belt. Now. Follow an imaginary straight line along the sky from those stars to that bright V shape cluster. That's the face of Taurus, the Bull. Do you see it?"

Another nod. "I think so."

"Good. That brightest star in the V is the eye of the Bull. It's called Aldeberan."

"I think I see it." June sounded excited.

"Okay. Straight out from Aldeberan is a group of about six, bright stars. That's the Pleiades Cluster."

"Why is it called The Seven Sisters if there are only six stars?"

"Ah. That's because on some nights, generally in the

wintertime, you can see the seventh star. The rest of the time, it hides."

"It's beautiful."

Roi had a hard time not blurting out that June was beautiful, too. Instead, she withdrew her arm and sat beside June on the cape.

"It is beautiful," she said. "It's also kind of sad."

"Sad?" June turned to her. "Why sad?"

"Because they say that Aldeberan, which is Arabic for 'the follower,' will forever chase Pleiades across the heavens."

"And never catch her?"

Roi shook her head.

June looked back at the sky.

"You're right," she said in a quiet voice. "That is sad."

CHAPTER EIGHT
Ev'ry Time We Say Goodbye

PICO AND SMOOCHIE volunteered to drive them to the airport and train station. June expressed concern about this idea at first, but when they arrived, she was relieved to see that Bruce was driving, and they'd be riding in his Toyota Highlander. Pico was going to be spending a few days with Bruce in Wilmington, so the trip wasn't too much out of their way.

Pauline wasn't working the desk when they stopped by to check out. Roi was surprised until June told her that Fay was taking her in today to have her procedure.

The boys suggested that they stop for breakfast on their way to Philadelphia, but Roi nixed that idea and said she'd rather just head straight to the airport. As a compromise, they hit a McDonald's drive through on their way out of town and got a bag of egg white McMuffins.

June was not a big fan of fast food, but she decided to give it a try. She was amazed to discover how flavorful and satisfying the breakfast sandwich was.

"This is really delicious."

"Ay ay, nurse? If you think this is good, you needs to try that Velveeta biscuit they's showing on TV all the time." Pico's nose was still out of joint because Bruce refused to stop at Hardee's.

Velveeta? June was fairly certain that would never happen. "That sounds . . . intriguing."

Roi looked at her and she shrugged.

"It's *delicious*." Pico slapped Bruce on the arm. "Smoochie won't never let me have any of the good stuff."

Bruce made eye contact with June in the rearview mirror.

"That's because the thing is made with canned cheese and fried bologna."

"Yo, Mr. Brainiac?" Pico snapped his fingers. "Velveeta ain't canned. Is in a *block*." He made the shape with his hands. "Just like your briefcase brain."

Roi waded into the conversation. "I, for one, wouldn't survive without fast food."

Pico slapped Bruce's arm again. "See?"

"Don't you cook?" Bruce asked Roi.

"I *can* cook, but I usually don't. It's just too much trouble for one person."

"That's too bad," June said.

Still, she had to admit that she felt irrationally pleased by Roi's revelation that she normally ate by herself.

"Why?" Roi asked. "Do you cook for yourself?"

"Of course."

"You and I are alike in that way, nurse." Bruce had taken to addressing June by Pico's moniker. "I could never survive on Bobbie's preteen palate."

"Preteen? *Hel-lo*." Pico pointed at his lap. "There ain't nothing preteen in *this* package."

Bruce looked at him. "You know what I meant."

Pico huffed. "And I know what you likes, too."

They rode along in silence for a few minutes. The sun was just beginning to creep up over the horizon. The landscape around them was a maze of wetlands and coastal streams. Bright yellow and orange-red morning light reflected off the patches of water that flanked the highway. This terrain, with its scrubby trees and sandy, flat elevation, wasn't one June would ever call pretty. Still, there was something about it that she found appealing. Maybe it was simply her respect for the sheer determination it took for anything growing here to inveigh against the rising sea level.

Once again, a tiny David struggled to stand his ground against the encroaching leviathan, Goliath.

She thought about the irony of that, especially as it related to her own clumsy and desperate attempt to maintain her footing in a rapidly changing, emotional landscape.

She continued to stare out the window and watch the terrain roll by.

No. This time, she wasn't as optimistic about David's odds. *Or her own.*

The car ate up the miles in what felt like record time. June watched the smattering of small towns slowly morph into subdivisions, business parks, and strip malls. Before she knew it, they were on I-95, and beginning to see signs for the Philadelphia airport.

"What time is your train?" Bruce asked.

"Not until eleven," she replied.

"I'm really sorry my flight leaves so early," Roi apologized. "I should've just hired a car."

June turned to her. "Don't be silly. I can use the time to work on my column."

"Ay. Like you won't has enough time on that train for *two days?*" Pico waved a finger around in tiny circles beside his ear. "I would go loco."

"No you wouldn't," Bruce added. "You'd just set up shop in the club car."

"Yes, because all them businessmen from Altoona is *such* good companies."

Roi laughed.

"*See?*" Pico turned in his seat to face Roi. "You's the smart one, bepi. You'll be back in Chi-town before the nurse's train gets outta the station."

Roi didn't say anything.

"What airline are you flying, Roi?" Bruce asked.

"American. I think it's terminal A."

"Ay ay, bepi. Terminal A is the one with the crab fries. You gotta gets some of them."

"Crab fries?" Roi asked.

"Sí. At Chickie's and Pete's."

Bruce shook his head. "Take my advice, Roi. Walk on by."

"Oh, so *now* you's Miss Dionne Warwick?" Pico fluttered his hand up and down. "You gonna starts wearin' the dress, too?"

"Shut up, Bobbie."

June smiled and glanced over at Roi and realized that Roi had been staring at her. June thought she looked . . . thoughtful. Perplexed, even. Certainly preoccupied.

"Are you all right?" she asked, in a quiet voice.

Roi took a moment to answer. "I'm fine. Just thinking about everything that happened this weekend."

Everything?

June felt a twinge of panic. "It was pretty . . . remarkable."

Roi raised an eyebrow, and June regretted her word choice immediately.

"I mean . . . *extraordinary*," she corrected.

Oh god, that was even worse. Now Roi was smiling at her. She shook her head. "I don't know what I mean."

"It's okay." Roi touched the top of her hand. "I get it."

She sighed. "I'm glad."

Roi gave her hand a warm squeeze before releasing it.

"Yo, bepi?" Pico pointed with great animation at an exit sign. "Look. *Chester.*" He cackled. "You wanna get off and go for a rides down memory lane?"

Chester? June was amazed. Had it only been three days ago that they had been here? Had it only been *four* days ago that they had left Chicago? She felt like time had stood still during this trip—like she'd lived a lifetime in the last four days.

"No thanks," Roi replied. She looked at June. "We've already had enough excitement for one trip."

June felt herself flush. *Make that two lifetimes . . .*

"Suit yourself," Pico said. "But don't say I didn't offers."

A few minutes later, Bruce exited the highway and navigated toward the airport campus.

"Just drop me off at departures," Roi said. "Don't worry about trying to park."

Even at this early hour, the airport was humming with

travelers. Bruce pulled over near the signs for American Airlines.

"Bepi! Look!" Pico shrieked. "It's the Lesbanese from the hotel. I recognize the tool belts."

Roi rolled her eyes. "Great. Just what I needed."

"Oh, bepi . . . is she gonna be glads to see you. And look? She ain't walking the Duke no more, neither."

"Hey, Bruce?" Roi asked. "How about you pull up a ways so I can use the other entrance?"

"Roger."

Bruce eased back out into traffic and found another spot to pull into about fifty feet further down the terminal. He turned on his blinkers and hit a switch that popped open the trunk. They all got out of the car and waited while Roi retrieved her bags.

"Thanks for the ride," Roi said to Bruce. "And for everything else, too."

They shook hands.

She held out her hand to Pico, and he wagged a finger at her.

"Oh, no you don't, bepi. I don't gets no handshake instead of a kiss."

Roi sighed and stepped forward to give Pico a peck on the cheek, but at the last second, Pico shifted his head and kissed Roi, square on the lips.

"Oh, nurse," he gushed when they parted. "I sees now why you likes the young stuff." He fanned himself. "Your boi got some luscious lipses."

Bruce rolled his eyes and took hold of Pico's elbow. "Come on, Bobbie. Let's get in the car."

Pico shook him off. "Not until she says goodbye to the nurse."

Roi and June exchanged nervous glances.

"Come on, come on, you two." Pico snapped his fingers at them. "You gots to hug it out in the airport."

Roi hesitated.

"Sorry, Roi." Bruce sighed. "He's right. It's a binding social contract."

June could tell that Roi was torn about what to do.

"Oh, for god's sake. What on earth is the matter with you two? I've said more heartfelt goodbyes to lab rats."

June and Roi exchanged shocked glances.

Was that Pico?

Bruce chuckled. "I guess Dr. Brooks finally decided to put in an appearance."

Dr. Brooks ignored him. He was too busy waving his hands to direct June and Roi together. "In this lifetime, if you don't mind?"

Roi gave June an apologetic smile. She slid her camera bags off her shoulder and set them on the pavement beside her suitcase.

June could feel her heart pounding as Roi stepped toward her.

This is it, she thought. *We'll say goodbye and it will be over. It'll be quick and simple, and in a few minutes, my world will make sense again.*

Roi reached out for her.

Oh, god. Who am I kidding?

They held each other for a moment. June closed her eyes and tried desperately to recall a time in her life before she knew how wonderful this felt. But she couldn't. She couldn't think about anything. She was taking all the stamina she possessed just to remain standing.

Roi slowly loosened her arms and drew back. They looked at each other.

This is it, she thought. *This is goodbye.*

Roi slowly released her. "So I guess I'll see you back at the paper?"

June nodded. She was having a hard time summoning up a response that wouldn't sound inane.

"We can . . . maybe . . . meet and go over the photos? I

mean . . . if you want to. I guess." Roi took a step backward and ran into her suitcase. "Shit."

"I'd like that." June finally found her voice.

Roi picked up her camera bags. "You would?"

June nodded. "A lot."

"Me, too."

They smiled at each other.

"Okay," Roi said. "I guess I need to go. You have a safe trip home."

June nodded again. "I will."

Roi stared at her for another moment. Then she took hold of her roller bag.

"Thanks, guys. It's been great." She looked at June again. "Really."

She turned on her heel and headed toward the entrance to the terminal.

The emptiness June felt was palpable. But she knew it would subside in time. It had to.

They got back into the car, and Bruce pulled away from the curb.

June fought an impulse to turn around.

She chided herself for her weakness. Then she questioned her determination.

Oh, this is just ridiculous, she thought. *We're not in Nineveh. I won't turn into a pillar of salt if I look back.*

Someone blew a horn at Bruce. While the boys were preoccupied flipping off a shuttle driver and dodging two pedestrians who were juggling about nineteen suitcases, she gave in and looked back toward the terminal.

Her heart missed a beat.

Roi was still standing there, leaning against a stone pillar, watching as their car pulled away.

CHAPTER NINE
Early Autumn

"WERE YOU AWARE that Miss Lord had attempted suicide in high school?"

Emily looked at the bloody tissue in her hand. "Yes. I knew."

"I received the autopsy report several hours ago. Your friend's death was ruled a drowning. No foreign substances were found in her body and the only unusual marks that were visible were some old scars on each of her wrists. We checked on it and found out that she had attempted suicide when she was sixteen. It seems some girl she thought she was in love with had been sent away to a private school by her parents. I imagine it was an attempt to separate them."

A fly was buzzing around inside the waiting room. No matter how many times she chased it, it kept returning to land on the pages of her book. She sighed and shooed it away again, and thought about going to the snack bar to get another cup of coffee. But she'd had too much already, and she didn't want to add to her agitation. Already she was feeling far too anxious and keyed-up.

"Shortly after the girl left town, Allison's father found her in one of the bathrooms. She'd slit her wrists. I suppose you already know the whole story." He studied her for a reaction.

June lowered the book and drummed her fingers against the arm of the bench.

This was ridiculous. Why was she finding it so hard to concentrate?

> "So what are you trying to say?" she said angrily. "All gays and lesbians are innately suicidal? Depressed? Ambivalent about their sexuality? Is that it? Except that Allison was nothing like that. When she was sixteen years old, she fell in love. It happens all the time. Poets write about the joys of young love. The problem was, she happened to fall in love with another woman."

June put the book down in frustration.

Of all the books on earth, why had Letty given her *this* one to read? What in the world had she been thinking?

June sighed. She knew precisely what Letty had been thinking. Letty, it seemed, knew her better than she knew herself.

She decided to try again.

> "Everyone in her family told her she was either sick or sinful. It's quite a dilemma for a sixteen-year-old. She knew she was neither of those things, but it's terrifying to be different."

June slammed the book shut.

This was impossible. It felt like a conspiracy.

She looked at her watch. Nine forty-five. She had another solid hour to wait until they began to board her train for Pittsburgh.

Then what?

Then she'd have seventeen more hours of solitude until she reached Chicago.

*"Well," he said, "I was sent over here to give you something.
A special delivery kind of thing."*

Maybe once she was aboard and actually on her way, things would settle down and she'd be able to regroup. Of course she would. She'd be able to put this emotional rollercoaster behind her and get some perspective. That's really all she needed: *perspective.*

It was uncomplicated, really.

Wasn't it?

"Excuse me, ma'am."

June jumped. She hadn't noticed the porter approaching her.

"I'm sorry, ma'am," he apologized. "I didn't mean to scare you."

"No, no. That's all right," she said. "I was just lost in thought."

"Yes, ma'am. I understand." The older man smiled at her. "These old benches are just made for that."

"I think you're right," June agreed.

"Are you Miss June Magee, R.N.?" he asked.

June nodded. "Yes, I am."

"Well," he said, "I was sent over here to give you something. A special delivery kind of thing."

June noticed for the first time that he was carrying some kind of tray covered with a white napkin.

"Special delivery?" June was perplexed. "For me?"

"Yes, ma'am." He handed her the tray and touched the brim of his cap. "You have a nice ride now, ma'am." He left her and wandered off toward the door that led to the boarding platform.

June felt confused as she watched him walk away.

This is certainly very strange.

She lifted the edge of the napkin and took a peek at what lay beneath it.

It was a small box. A small *yellow* box . . . with big brown letters.

Oh my god.

June pulled the napkin all the way off.

Milk Duds? Who on earth?

She quickly scanned the concourse. All she saw were the same droves of nameless, faceless people who had been milling around and hurrying around and killing time in there ever since she arrived, more than two hours ago.

She looked down at the box again. A tiny card stuck out beneath one of its corners. She pulled it out and read it.

Dibs on the bottom bunk.

June closed her eyes and smiled.

She looked more carefully about the cavernous space and saw her leaning against the information booth beneath the Solari departure board.

Roi was looking right at her. She collected her bags and made her way across the polished marble hall that could have doubled as an indoor football field.

June watched her approach with wonder.

Roi reached the bench and gave June a shy smile.

"Is this seat taken?"

*She looked more carefully about the cavernous space
and saw her leaning against the information booth
beneath the Solari departure board.*

ABOUT THE AUTHORS

ANN McMAN is the award-winning author of four novels, *Jericho, Dust, Aftermath*, and *Hoosier Daddy*, and the short story collections *Sidecar* and *Three*. She was inducted into the Royal Academy of Bards Hall of Fame in 2011, and awarded the Alice B. Lavender Certificate for Outstanding Debut Novel. She has won two Goldies, as well as several Rainbow Awards and Lesbian Fiction Readers Choice Awards. Ann was one of 25 emerging authors invited to write an introductory essay for the Lambda Literary Foundation's 25th anniversary publication. Her novel, *Hoosier Daddy*, which was co-authored with wife Salem West, was a 2014 Lambda Literary Award Finalist.

SALEM WEST spent twenty-five years in Washington, D.C. doing murky things that other people didn't want or know how to do. In 2011 she retired and founded her breakout blog, The Rainbow Reader, which combines homespun essays with queer-centric perspectives in book reviews that cover a wide swath of mostly lesbian literature. Her first novel, *Hoosier Daddy*, which was co-authored with wife Ann McMan, was a 2014 Lambda Literary Award Finalist.

BARRETT grew up in the Chicago suburbs. Art and music fueled an overactive imagination that eventually channeled into a flair for the dramatic and a dream of acting. Life and times deferred that dream but offered a new challenge. After her ten-year class reunion, Barrett started nursing school and a career with endless challenges and learning opportunities, which spanned thirty years, several jobs, and great travels.

After relocating to New Mexico, Barrett set down roots and fell helplessly into a new passion—writing. Her first book,

Damaged in Service was a finalist for a Golden Crown Literary Society Award. It is the first of a four book series that includes: *Defying Gravity*, *Dispatched With Cause*, and *Deliver Me* (2015). Other works include *Balefire*, *Flights of Fancy*, and *Windy City Mistletoe*.

She is a member of the Golden Crown Literary Society, Romance Writers of America, RWA Published Author Network, Land of Enchantment Romance Authors, Petroglyph Guild, WOA Readers Group, and TOTS. She is founder of the Western Women Writers of New Mexico annual event.

About the Illustrator

Biz gets by with a little help from her friends.
Pictured clockwise from left are Lucy, Marley, Allie, Maddie, Gracie, and Max.

Accomplished illustrator, model, and steampunk aficionado, Hayden "Biz" Sharpe holds a BFA in Studio Art with a concentration in painting from Appalachian State University.

She can be reached at bizsharpe@gmail.com.

CPSIA information can be obtained
at www.ICGtesting.com
Printed in the USA
FFOW01n1557180315
11900FF